Danishing
Poems

将·逝·之·诗

[冰岛] 古戈尔·权斯莱特

编著

星蓝出版社

将逝之诗
contents

中文版序

　　二十多年前，我出版了这本小册子，内容不是很丰富，但足以显示出我工作的意义。现在，此书要在中国出版了。在这本书第一次出版的时候，因为时间原因我并没有收录太多的亚洲诗歌，所以在此之后我一直在亚洲搜集资料，希望能有一天可以补全这个空缺。中国是一个文明古国，有着古老的历史和博大精深的文化，这也就意味着，中国也有很多正在消亡的诗歌。我希望我的书能够唤起人们对于消逝的诗歌的兴趣，将这些文字转化为我们共同的记忆。

　　为了更好的阅读效果，整本书的中文翻译皆出自我手，因为有些语言过于小众，担心会有漏译、错译的现象发生。

　　希望中国的读者们能够享受并喜欢这本书。

古戈尔·权斯莱特

2019年4月

序 言

当我写下这些文字的时候，孟加拉湾湿热的海风正在吹拂。几天前，一场台风刚刚过去，将我在海边购下的木屋摧毁，里面保存的诗歌荡然无存。每到面对失败的时候，我会开始想念我的家乡冰岛，但是我知道，我最终的目标，是尽可能多地记录、保存即将逝去的诗句，和它们所蕴含的光怪陆离的人类故事。

这些伟大而奇妙的文学作品，或因为其语言过于冷门，或因为其创作地过于偏僻，很多都面临着消失、被人遗忘的危险。这些作品的珍贵，除了其文学价值之外，还有其背后所隐藏的故事。每一个小小的细节都是人类共同的记忆，不管这些记忆是多么的微不足道，他们终究都是属于全人类的，每一个句子，每一个字符，每一个片段都不能被抛弃。作为一个语言学家，在过去的几十年里，我一直被一个目标所驱使，那就是搜集世界各地的即将失传的诗歌，并且尽我所能地挖掘他们所蕴含的意义。从我的家乡开始，我已经走遍了欧洲、非洲，和一部分的亚太地区，搜集了无数有趣的值得被铭记的作品。我知道我做得还不够多，但是至少挽救了一部分作品，记录下了一些人类共同记忆的片段。

这本小集子是我从目前已经记录下来的、浩如烟海的消逝的诗歌和注释中挑选出来的精品，量很少，但是有其价值，望读者朋友们鉴赏。

在我为这本诗集搜集资料的同时，启发我进行这一浩大工程的那位作家，也是我的好友——斯多利·马什，出版了他最伟大的作品之一——《失落的故事》。在这本书中，他搜集了来自世界各地大量濒临失传的民间故事，并对其进行了加工，以一个个精巧的中短篇小说呈现。这本书的出版以及大获成功对我当时正在做的工作无疑是具有极大英国著名学者、皇家学院的威利斯爵士于昨日被发现死于自己的家中，死因不明。威利斯爵士在此前数个月闭门不出。去世前两天将冰岛语言学家古戈尔·权斯来特先生邀请至自己的家中讨论学术问题。随后古戈尔先生打电话报警，声称威利斯爵士猝死。警方到达时大门敞开着，爵士的车被开走，房子里没有其他人。爵士的助手帮助警方清点了财产，发现并没有强行盗窃的痕迹，不过家中丢失了一些藏品，包括几本古书、一套中国瓷器、一些波斯挂毯和一个黑色的三角文物。

一张纸条被留下，上面用一种古埃及文及方言写道："他还活着；真相比生命更重要；真正死去的不是人们想象的那个；将会失去眼睛。"

古戈尔先生目前行踪不明。

激励作用的。因此借序言，我要向斯多利·马什先生致谢，并以《失落的故事》中的一段话作为本书的开始：

人类就像在沙滩上奔跑的孩子，而文字就是他的脚印。孩子跑向远方的同时，他的脚印正在被抹除。而我所做的，无非是建造一座沙做的大坝，暂时守护那一点属于过去的脚印，为孩子勾勒出他的旅程。与自然抗争是不自量力的，沙做的大坝终有一天会倒塌，我所记录下的故事也终究会被遗忘，但是至少那昙花一现的印记，会让孩子记起他出发的地方，从而毫无负担地奔向远方。

古戈尔·权斯莱特

1995年11月

将逝之诗

·
·
·

欧　洲　诗　歌

一切工作的起源都滥觞于我的家乡冰岛。由这里出发，我花了将
近十年的时间走遍了几乎整个欧洲，像候鸟一样从北到南又从
西到东，不停地搜寻那些失落的歌谣。欧洲的诗歌风格跨度极
广，从古老的神话到简短的箴言无所不包。在此章节，我选择了
三十六首具有代表性的诗歌，以展现这些将逝之诗的风采。

·
·
·

[1]

欺诈虚弱

乞讨权力

我们的国王

寿命长

ooo　　1982年的某个暖和的冬日午后，我在丹麦北部的海滩上闲逛，偶然发现了一块刻着文字的石碑。我将这些文字临摹了下来，带给我在丹麦皇家科学院的好友——奥拉夫博士（他一直以精于研究奇怪的历史细节而著称）看。他十分激动地告诉我，我这些偶然的收获证明了他的一个推测，那就是丹麦曾经有过一位"被隐藏的国王"——康哈三又二分之一世。这首小小的讽刺诗讲述的正是他的故事，它用非常简短的句子概述了他的一生。

　　生活在12世纪的康哈本是一个渔夫，靠在赌场中诈骗一位无法站起来的老人起家。康哈以他的花言巧语，和一点小小的花招，赢得了这位老人全部的财产。后来，他偶遇了当时的国王——瓦尔德马一世。具体的过程人们不得而知，但最后康哈通过厚颜无耻的坚持赢得了当一天国王的机会，日子可以由他自行选择。于是当康哈得知瓦尔德马一世于伏尔丁堡猝死时，他立即使用了自己乞讨来的这个机会，在新王继位前加冕为王。大臣们用怜悯的目光望着他，并嘲讽他失去了理智。但是当康哈拿出先王手谕时，大臣们沉默了。他们经过讨论，觉得让康哈荒诞地登基可以平复国内悲伤的气氛，并且可以"让他吸收走先王暴毙的不幸气息"。康哈登基之后，人们对他满是不屑，但他在一天之内（具体过程不得而知）说服了所有的大臣，让他的统治可以延续到他的死亡。康哈三又二分之一世的政权少有人承认，大部分人都效忠于瓦尔德马的儿子，对这个他们一手创造的笑话视而不见，但王国倒是奇妙地维持了很长时间的和平。康哈在位七十年整，死的时候将近一百岁。因为他的故事过于荒诞，后人决定抹消掉他的存在。

康哈的一生就是这样，有意思的是，他一直吹嘘自己有很多珍宝（当然，是从那位可怜的老人那里得到的）。据他所说，这里面有世界上最大的绿宝石，有长得像鲸鱼一样的金块，记载着"世界上所有灵魂"的书籍，还有镶嵌着三角形"纯粹的火焰"的项链。当然，没有人见到过它们。所以在那个石碑被发现的地方，有这么一句俗语："康哈国王的珍宝"，指代被拙劣地编造出来的谎言。

[2]
为什么碰撞朗姆酒？
低沉的羞耻喷涌而出
血腥的死亡郁郁葱葱
好酒！好酒！

∘∘∘　　这首诗是我在对纳瓦拉王国桑乔三世时期阿方索将军墓葬的一次
发掘中发现的。那是 1976年的夏天，因为我对巴斯克语有一定的了
解，考古队的负责人卡洛斯教授委托我去辨认一批刚刚发掘出来的文
献。工作之余，我查看了他们发掘出的其他文物，其中一个密封完好
的陶瓶引起了我的注意。这个陶瓶大约三十厘米高，有一个五厘米长
的细颈，瓶身上刻满了弯曲的条纹。我在这些弯曲的条纹中辨认出了
一些花体的巴斯克语句子，也就是各位读者所阅读到的这首诗。

　　这首诗的第一句中提到了一种酒类，如果直译的话可以译为
"莫米克"，因为"莫米克"的制作方法与我们所熟知的朗姆酒极
为相似，我在翻译时便自作主张使用了"朗姆酒"作为译文。而后
几句提到了血腥与死亡两个意象，因此，学者们推测这首诗是为阿方
索将军所领导的比利牛斯山战役的胜利而作。但是具体这首诗是将军
本人的作品还是由其身边大臣所赠，在其他更多的资料被发掘之前我
们就不得而知了。

[3]
和尚的灯
打开蓝色极地冰
它是真正的火花
在夜晚闪耀

○○○　　这首诗来自冰岛西北最寒冷的地区，因此其中对"和尚"的描述就显得有些奇怪。众所周知，冰岛之前为诺德信仰，后来转成基督教，几乎从未与佛教进行接触。我在当地寻求帮助的时候，遇到了一位历史学家伊瓦尔先生，我们在经过讨论之后理清了这么一条线索：在蒙古人西征的过程中，有大量蒙古后裔留在了现在伏尔加河流域（现俄罗斯卡尔梅克共和国境内）。据说利斯塔·阿勃拉姆，一位来自以色列的诺斯替教派信徒，于13世纪来到这里并定居了下来，诺斯替教与当地的泛灵信仰融合成了一种奇妙的宗教流派。后来16世纪土尔扈特人征服了这里，佛教又与之融合。

　　在17世纪，一位来自阿斯特拉罕（那附近的一座城市）的独眼商人，也是之前那个诺斯替信徒的后代，利斯塔·阿勃拉姆十二世，来到了冰岛，在西北方向的一座冰山旁建立了一座寺庙。当时的居民不了解其历史，便将他简单地称作"和尚"。他的一家人从此居住在了寺庙里。人们不喜欢这一家人，因为他们说话有严重的口音，且举止怪异：每一代利斯塔都会带着一个眼罩，他们解释为"家族传统"。在二战期间，据历史学家所描述，当地人目击到他的后代利斯塔·阿勃拉姆二十一世举着"橙红色的光"进入了他的寺庙，随后冰面裂开，发出淡淡的蓝光，整个寺庙就消失不见了，只剩下橙红色的火焰持续燃烧，昼夜不绝。我亲自到那个传说中的地址探索了一遍，甚至雇用了一位渔夫载我前往海里，尝试寻找这座寺庙的踪迹。但什么都没有发现，我唯一的收获是埋在浅海中的一块带链子的石头，石头上凹下去一个三角形的形状。这个也许是项链的东西被我收藏在家中，权当纪念。

　　鉴于没有其他的解释，我姑且将这个故事放在这里。

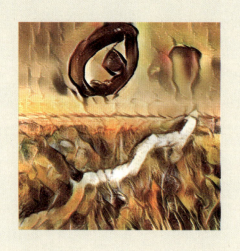

[4]

你好吗?

我是个鼹鼠

我挥挥手

抱着我的月亮

∘∘∘　　这首诗是在一个古旧的毛绒玩具标签上找到的，标签所属的毛绒
　　玩具已经找不到了，但是从诗句的内容推断，这个标签属于1856年到
　　1861年间风靡西班牙的漫画形象"月上鼹鼠"。

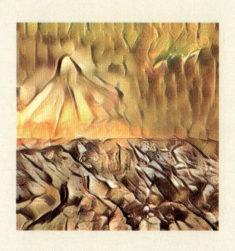

[5]

我们建议

您花七周时间

陷入死亡

现在正在向宇宙涌入一片大云

无论什么能量，我都是自由而死的

°°°　　17世纪前期的德国中部，大片土地仍然可以称得上是未开化
的。在这片土地上，潜藏着许多为了逃避战乱以及宗教的人们。讽刺
的是，在这里生活了不到二十年时间的他们中间竟然也形成了一个名
叫"殆沃克"（Die Wolke）的邪教教会。当时的人们相信，通过某
种能量转化手段，将逝之人是能够被转化成类似云状的物质（据现代
考古学家在德国南部地区的考证，转化过后的物质成分竟与月壤的成
分基本一致）并永远地化作宇宙长久不变的物质中的一分子。在这种
与安乐死极其相似的邪教仪式过程中，被转变的人会在长达五十天的
时间里被封锁在由用黑玛瑙镶嵌的大理石墙壁构成的狭窄空间里，只
通过一个方形的小窗口从外界拿取食物。

　　但是，被转化的人所享用的并不是什么盛宴，而是一种质感介
于橡胶和塑料之间的天然木本植物产物。虽然是天然产物，但这种物
质在后来并没有投入大量使用（无论是生产加工还是食用，因为它
似塑胶非塑胶的性质实在是不讨人喜爱），只是之后在大西洋的海滨
地区有小规模的使用。在最后的十天中，小窗口会被完全封死，里面

< 008 >

的人并不能与外界取得任何联系，因为仪式的执行者们相信，如果打开小窗口会使里面所贮存的能量泄漏出来。至于在这十天中，这个牢笼中具体发生了什么，我们就不得而知了。在第四十九天的深夜，牢笼会被打开，转而进入长达十二个小时的"能量释放期"。据传闻，在这期间，逝者所转化成的物质会通过能量通道散射到宇宙中去，就此纳入永恒（令人哭笑不得的是，就在几年以前，唯一尚存的大理石墙壁下被发现有向南挖掘的痕迹）。由于这个邪教组织领导人高超的才智，这样恐怖的邪教仪式被宣传为每一个教会成员都梦想着的最终归宿，这才有了这首诗的由来。不幸的是，直到每一次仪式的结束，人们都认为逝者是通过类似安乐死的方法平静地被转化为宇宙中"永恒"的物质。

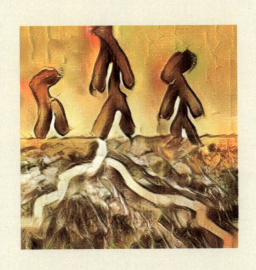

[6]

大海在岛上飞行

月亮变成了白宫

没有故事的洞穴

充满闪电的山峰

你看看周围的镜子

这是噩梦般的粉红色

在我面前的人是精神焕发的

他在我面前疯狂

他没有生气

相反，这是一位孤独的圣人

°°°　　希腊文诗歌。被发现于一根石柱上，于4世纪被刻下。大约描写
了一位游客去会见一位异教先知后所经历的迷幻之旅。众所周知，当
时大量的宗教行为都会使用致幻剂，这位游客应当是喝下了先知给他
的所谓的"神奇药水"。可以明显地看出，游客起初认为这位先知是
"疯狂"的，但后来他的形象转变成了"孤独的圣人"，药效可见一
斑。诗中"粉红色的镜子"估计也是仪式的一部分。

　　有意思的是，石柱的另一边有几句对于这位先知的描写，原文如
下：

　　"他衣衫褴褛，瘦骨嶙峋，无法行走；但是他的眼睛 ——哦！
他的眼睛是如此的深邃，令人难以捉摸，仿佛在凝视着海底的深渊一

　　般，可能那就是为什么他只有一只眼睛的原因，伟大的诸神无法忍受
有一双这样的眼睛……"

　　这段描写的下方，有另外一句话：

　　"我自由了。"

[7]

凌晨四点

抬头看看自由的阳光

无论谁受伤，你都有不可动摇的奉献精神

无论如何要修复相同的错误

∘∘∘　　这首诗用俄语书写，被发现于阿斯特拉罕城郊一家旅店古老的橡
木门上，时间大约是17世纪。全诗体现出了极大的决心："无辜而死
的灵魂们，请原谅我，这是为了[难以辨认]"。难以辨认的符号应当
属于诺斯替教派的某个分支。

< 012 >

[8]
不要犹豫杀死他们
不要隐藏他们的拇指
让他们保持丝状
让他们满意

°°° 　在中世纪斯堪的纳维亚的北部，一帮被称作"栝特"的刽子手
们专门收取钱财来杀死主顾们的仇人。在人倒在雪地后的几十分钟以
内，由于脑部的血液会保持一段时间的温度，所产生的水蒸气会凝结
成类似冰霜之类的物质将头发粘结在一起，而侦探们能够凭借此推断
出受害人倒地的大概时间。为了不让侦探们从受害人身上获取蛛丝马
迹，刽子手们想方设法地让受害人的头发不被冰霜粘结在一起。出于
某种炫耀的目的，刽子手们在用裹尸布覆盖住受害者身体的时候并不
会掩盖手部。这两点也成为栝特帮内部评判生意好坏的重要标准。

[9]

鱼人决定再次找到并改变它

因为它远远不是塑料制品

它还在的时候，它到处旅行

并开设了一家进口的小公司

但时间是邪恶行为的牺牲品

大部分海洋终于开始死亡

鱼人找到了它

它是一条鱼

味道像海的鱼

ooo　　这首诗被发现于莫洛克海鱼罐头厂的员工手册中《莫洛克海鱼罐
头厂简史》一章。这个罐头厂于1928年关停，原因是有大量消费者认
为该厂使用塑料伪造鱼肉售卖。

[10]

我有一份珍贵的礼物

是一个咆哮愤怒的懦夫

在海边的一块丝绸

和一只漂亮小鸟的红色羽毛

他飞得很远很远

让它吸吮你的眼睛

○○○　　这首诗是在法国尼斯的萨雷雅集市上的一个古董摊位上找到的。逛这种古董摊是我的一大爱好，因为我经常可以在这里找到一些很有趣的故事，而我又往往是唯一一个看得懂这些故事的人。这首诗便是在这样的情况下被发现的。那是一个9月的周一，萨雷雅集市每周的古董市场都是周一，所以我一早就来到了这里。天气有些凉，我打了个喷嚏，正在我掏手帕的时候，我看到一个摊位上有一块漂亮的红色丝绸手帕，上面隐隐地绣着一些字迹。我走近观察，发现上面的字竟是一首冰岛语的诗，就是你们读到的这一首。在法国发现一个绣着自己母语的古董着实是一件罕事，于是我便向摊位的老板问起这件古董。

　　老板叫作皮埃尔，是尼斯本地人，年轻的时候是一名私家侦探。这块手帕属于他曾经协助调查的一个案子的死者，而死者的家属把这块手帕送给了他。据皮埃尔所说，那个死者的死状十分奇特，他坐在书桌前，这块手帕就端正地摆在他的腿上，而一支红色的羽毛笔深深

地插在了他的眼眶里。我给皮埃尔把这首诗翻译了一遍，他愣了几秒，眼神里似乎是疑惑又似乎是恍然大悟，待我再问他关于这起案件的信息时，他便什么也不愿说了。

[11]

你是最后一个人

并在房间里死亡

你这只眼睛眨了眨眼

突然

有些事情正在发生

是的，你的头发

唤醒并控制世界

○○○　　"栝特"帮为何在其最壮大的时刻突然消失，想必整个世界都不
　　　　得而知。我们所知道的全部，就是所有有关它的文字记录。这首诗是
　　　　栝特帮内部流传下来的最后一首诗，据说刽子手在处理受害者的头发
　　　　时发生了不可思议的事情。当然，这只是出自侦探之口。然而，当对
　　　　这个案子进行进一步分析的时候，专门负责处理栝特的探长彼得·克
　　　　朗突然宣布结案了。

[12]
一直到六月的爆炸

在击中散射的罪恶之后

这宇宙中的人听到了

最后一个声音

他走得很远很远

去哪儿了？

○○○　　俄语诗歌，出现在1908年6月30日通古斯大爆炸前一天的《博特

加里报》上，作者未知。

[13]
骑士的机械革命的杰作
用黑烟摧毁城市
告诉你们，你们要沉溺于沉默
然后教皇去世了

∘∘∘　　这里的一切开始于公元64年，永恒之城罗马在尼禄的统治下遭遇了一场大火。火从竞技场开始烧起，持续了六天七夜，全罗马十四个行政区中只有四个毫发无损。尼禄得知之后暴怒，认为这是基督徒的阴谋，开始迫害基督徒。他所不知道的是，有居民在火源地——竞技场的中心发现了一些奇怪的东西——齿轮，无比精密的齿轮。

　　我在罗马城逗留的时候，设法找到了一位神通广大的收藏家，就是他将那些齿轮拿给我："你可以看到它无比精密的工艺，像这样大小的齿轮只能在18世纪后找到……从它的机械结构来判断，真的很难相信这是在古罗马时期被发现的，看这充满韧性的纽带，还有这覆盖着主体的玻璃，难以置信！"他还向我展示了一本古书，是当时罗马城内一位居民的日记。在他的日记里，我发现了这首诗。这是他在大火之后三年写下的，应当是用一种更加艺术化的手法体现出了他在大火前的经历。他写道："就在灾难发生的那天前，我见到了一名骑兵。他应当十分富有，因为他的全身几乎都被银色的盔甲覆盖着，暴露在外面的只有一些奇妙的机械结构和透明的物体……天色很晚，街上只有我一个人，他对我说要保持沉默，声音沙哑生涩，仿佛生锈的金属互相摩擦……"

　　那天的记录戛然而止，纸页上有烧焦的痕迹。这位居民逃过了一劫，但很不幸在随后对基督教徒的迫害中死亡。当时的教皇圣彼得也在这场运动中被害。

[14]

通往宇宙的道路

只不过是一间农舍

来自一个兰纳尔的遗迹

同样也是一个伟大的故事

○○○　　这首诗来自列支敦士登的当地传说。据说早在1723年，列支敦士登有一个隐秘的建筑师组织，这个组织内的成员由当时的天文学家和炼金术师组成，而这个组织的成员被称作"兰纳尔"。据说这是一间建在半山腰的农舍，而推开农舍的门便可以看到月亮上最细小的纹理。传说中这间屋子的遗址在20世纪被当地人发现了，但是房屋内空空如也，只有一些玻璃的残片和大型装置的痕迹，因此科学家推测诗中所述的可能是依靠某种光学手段达到的效果。

[15]

早上沉默

傍晚

给它一个答案

○○○ 　这是法国19世纪曾经流行过很短一段时间的"自填式百科全书"的广告语。这种百科全书里只有各个条目的标题而没有其下的内容，因此人们需要在早上挑选一个词条，并在一天的探索后将该词条的具体内容填充完整。但是由于工作量过于庞大，这种"自填式百科全书"的风潮很快就过去了，只有它精妙的广告词留存了下来。

[16]
尝试消隐
了解变幻莫测
规则不存在

沙漠创作的话语
在冰上漂浮
令人钦佩和多山

○○○　　这首诗曾刊登于18世纪前期东欧流行的《沃克报》。当欧洲的
科学还没有发展到很高的水平时，一些人想通过发明隐身药投机取
巧，以逃避兵役和税务，不法分子也想借此机会从警察的视野里永远
消失。可笑的是，总有些人认为自己成功发明了隐身药，于是便喝了
下去并开始自己的环球旅行，殊不知自己的每一首诗、每一篇札记，
以及一丝不挂的自己都能被世人所见。

[17]

有时一本书静静地睡着了

风轻轻地呼吸着空气

它将慢慢打开花瓣和眼睑，如威尼斯玫瑰

但他们看不到任何东西

木星蓝色的灵魂像天鹅绒一样柔软

有时在阳光下度过一整天的精华

每一朵云都有自己的竖琴

在高云边缘闪耀的颜色

人们对这令人印象深刻的光芒感到惊讶

他们闭着眼睛

严肃地凝视着

阳光在海上爆发

火炮，烟花和火药！

然后今晚湍流的光线平静下来

地平线将是圆的，美丽的，蓝色的

在里面，它包含了世界的闪闪发光的全景

但是，死岛永远不会复活

这就是生命的意义

○○○　　　希腊文诗歌，具体年代不可考。描述了诺斯替教派某分支教会的一本书籍，它记载着世界上所有有罪的灵魂。据说在未来的末日审判中（被信徒称作"死亡之日"）会被用于衡量人一生的善恶。

诗的第一段以奇幻的笔触描绘了书籍的样貌，其中"木星蓝色的灵魂"一句体现出了此教派万物有灵论的思想；第二段应当描写的是死亡之日的模样；最后一段将其升华，发表了对生命意义的一番言论，具体的内涵很难考证。

P.S.有意思的是，在这个分支教会中，审判日并不是"最终的"，而是重复出现的，但可以知道的是，每次出现都会造成灾难。

[18]

头痛!

头疼得厉害!

他说头痛

从来没有祸害

如果他不傻

他肯定在说谎

因为我的弱小灵魂

即将死亡

∘∘∘　这首诗是我1967年在德国旅行的时候在一处17世纪初被建造的
德国城堡内发现的。城堡的主人叫奥古斯都,是当时的一个传奇人
物,因为他与一些在当地失踪的社会名流在失踪前保持着很好的关
系。这首诗发现于这座城堡的地窖的密室内,这个密室的发现是因为
其外墙上有一块松动的砖被曾经的一位游客无意中取了下来。打开密
室后,考古学家发现这个密室的正式入口在城堡周边的一处水井内,
密室内除了这首诗什么也没有发现,因此无从推测密室的功能。

[19]

在某个世界

一半人从核心吸收了光伏压力

鉴于伟大的社会

他没有改变

人们使用唯一的声音松了一口气

在那个世界里，他可能已经死了

○○○　　这首诗写于1939年，当时正值纳粹德国的鼎盛时期，而这首诗
的作者是当时纳粹的一名科学家，巴尔杜·埃德曼博士。作者可能用
这首诗影射了当时纳粹德国领袖意志取代个人思考的社会现象，而诗
中的"他"被怀疑是作者本人。据埃德曼博士的助手埃克哈德·泽莫
曼的日记记录，埃德曼博士于该诗写作后第二年逃至美国。

[20]
深秋的细寒
扭曲苍白的天空
数千名学生匆匆走过
弯腰抵抗微风

石墙，看着他的脸
他是追求加速的追逐者
法老刺穿了他
他向法老的教导投降了
然后吱吱作响

∘∘∘　　1981年，我受邀参加冰岛大学的70周年校庆，听几位1944年毕业的冰岛大学校友谈起了这首诗。这首诗是这几位同学在那起轰动全校的命案后创作的。

　　因为冰岛大学1940年才刚刚建立校舍，所以学校出资从欧洲的一些博物馆借来了一些展品在新校舍的地下室里展出，供学生学习。这些展品包括大英博物馆的一个埃及石棺，几枚印度宝石戒指，法国罗浮宫的几幅画和奥地利盔甲博物馆的几套带长矛的盔甲，都是些不怎么特别但是又在冰岛平时看不到的东西。这几位校友刚好1940年入学，因此赶上了这个仅仅开放了一周就被迫结束的展览。

　　当天的情景就如诗的第一节，天空是一片白，有几丝微风吹过，

命案发生后，所有的学生第一时间被带离了教学楼。虽说没有亲眼看到现场，谣言还是很快传出来了。据说死者是学校田径队的一名成员，他对历史一窍不通，曾经在学校里多次质疑四大文明古国的存在。而讽刺的是，他正死在那架埃及石棺旁，身体被一支来自奥地利的盔甲的长矛刺穿了。警察事后将这件事定性为一起"凶手还没有抓到的谋杀"，但是同届的很多学生都认为这是来自法老的诅咒，从这几位校友的诗里我们便可以读出这一点。

[21]

我一点也不知道啊

你的杆子锁在箱子里

有一个黑客和小贩

我不同意见面

○○○　　被发现在柏林。时间是1988年，冷战期间，当时的德国是两方
　　　情报站拉锯的前线。这其实并不是一首诗，而是一段支离破碎的录
　　　音，被人记录下来。当地人告诉我这是一个间谍窃听警察局的审问记
　　　录下来的对话。一三两句是被逮捕的人所说的，二四两句是警察所
　　　说。"杆子"是东德地下市场的黑话，指代步枪。

[22]

请等一下

在湖崩溃之前

沉默的第二次霜冻

奠定了玫瑰的目标

永远不要让他们知道

你讨厌太阳

哦，是的，那个时候

我是太阳

○○○　　俄语诗歌，被发现于乌拉尔山的石壁上。诗歌精妙无比，以太阳神的口吻讲述了一则当地神话的一部分：每当冬天来临的时候，在全世界最高的山峰上，会有一丛玫瑰长出，这花朵的生长和死亡周期恰好是整个冬天，在冬日最后的时间里，它的花瓣会随风飘落，在广袤无垠的大地上尝试寻找一本记载着罪人灵魂的书籍。每一片花瓣的到达都说明又会有九千八百人的灵魂受到审判。花瓣的飘落直到春天都不会停止，对应文中"在湖崩溃之前"（指解冻）。当地的村民告诉我，传说中有一年的冬天无比漫长，以至于花瓣飘落了仿佛无限之久。于是过了几年，东方的蒙古人到来了，军队杀死了许多的居民。人们都说那些人的死去正是因为有太多的花瓣飞到了书籍当中。

[23]

我记得今天早上

明媚的早晨

我跑在一些孩子身后

脚下是柔软的土壤和草地，在风中跳舞

太阳似乎对我们来说就像一种温柔的色彩

我们就像河边的羔羊一样

我们来到一个破旧的寺庙

我看到了一些伟大的神灵

这似乎已经持续了很长时间

然而，他们正在死去

那天晚上，暴风雨刚过去了

天空中的乌云像滚滚的烟雾

我坐在房子后面的池塘里，在潮湿的风景中

一个陌生的男人来找我

他有黑色的衣服

随着黑旗在黑暗的天空下移动

他说我应该继续这一天

这个无限宇宙中的特殊日子

然后我才认识到

这个冬天是永恒的

他们就像船

像我的静脉，我的脖子

我有很多缠绕的绳索，我永远无法解决

红罗宾死在金合欢树上

最后，我为自己而死

∘∘∘　　1990年，俄罗斯阿斯特拉罕的一座东正教堂要被拆除并重新修建，工人们在它的地基里发现了篆刻在银板上的这首诗，便请我去鉴定。我翻译了这首诗，并且发现了一个细节：地基的材料明显比教堂的古老、粗糙。应我的要求，他们仔细地清理干净了泥土，随后我发现被埋在地下的是一个诺斯替教派的聚会地点，后来修建的教堂是为了掩盖这里曾经存在过异端的痕迹。我的朋友，英国皇家学院的威利斯爵士提出，这首诗描写的可能是在他们信仰的审判日 ——死亡之日后发生的一些事情。上半段描写的是之前的美好生活，结尾处笔锋一转，叙述出了诸神正在死亡的事实，引出了死亡之日降临的描述。"暴风雨"暗指死亡之日，"乌云"和"烟雾"所指都应当是审判之后的惨状。穿着黑色衣服的陌生男人找到了叙述者，邀请他"继续无限宇宙中的特殊日子"。这句话在当地属于一个民间传说，据说一个独眼的黑衣男子会去狩猎年轻的男孩，问他们愿不愿意"继续无限宇宙中的特殊日子"，如果男孩同意的话，独眼人会用一种冒出橙红色火焰的法术夺走他的灵魂，将自己的意识灌入对方的躯体中，以达到永生的效果——可惜他的独眼会被永远保留。在每一次灵魂的转移之后，都会发生一次意外导致他的一只眼睛消失。

　　诗最后的内容比较好理解，讲述了一个因为预见到死亡之日的恐怖的人（也许是诗人自己）而绝望自杀的故事。"我有很多缠绕的绳索，我永远无法解决"明确地体现了主角正在经历的痛苦挣扎，静脉和脖子的意象也暗示了最后的结局。但是此诗还有一些令人费解的词语亟须解释。

罗宾鸟又名知更鸟，分布于世界各地。在当地卡尔梅克人的神话中，一只红色的罗宾鸟是他们的可汗与诸神战斗落败时拯救她的生灵，在本诗当中应是美好的象征，它在金合欢树上的死亡预示了诗人内心中美好一面的消逝。

金合欢树原产于热带美洲，直至现在也只能在热带地区发现。即使阿斯塔拉罕在俄罗斯境内已经十分靠南，依旧无法种植金合欢。但是，在我搜寻资料的时候，发现了一位来自格鲁吉亚的学者的记载，他声称此地区在12世纪经历过一次非正常的气温升高，其余波持续了长达三十年。金合欢树虽然生长周期极为漫长，在这个窗口期也是有可能出现的。所以诗中的"金合欢"可能并不是活着的树，而是从那个时代传下来的工艺品。

永恒的冬天是一则神话，应当由乌拉尔地区传播到这里，描述了神灵是怎样以夺取阳光来惩罚一位尝试挑战他的权威的英雄，漫长的冬天造就了无数无辜生灵的死亡。此用典在这里的用意不明，有可能只是为了炫耀作者的学识，或者暗示死亡之日比永恒的冬天更可怕。

P.S.当地有关奇妙法术的传言很多，除此之外还有"吞下珍珠以永生"或"将镜子漆成粉红色以治愈疾病"的民间怪谈，我的好友斯多利·马什的《失落的故事》一书中有更加详细的记载。

[24]

在桥梁后面

是赤裸的霜

黑暗的季风

我死于阳光

○○○　　1832年，为清除莱茵河的岩石对航运带来的影响，相关人士决定在德国宾根炸出两条航道。在第二条航道的开辟中，一座桥梁被摧毁。这座桥梁的四角各有一只石像鬼，这在桥梁设计上是不多见的。在没有经过文物部门批准的情况下，这座桥的桥面被炸毁，四个石像鬼被砸碎，这件事于1982年才被披露出来。据相关文件显示，工人在这座桥东南角的石像鬼头中发现了一张羊皮纸，上面写着这首诗。

[25]

一种哲学

一种语言

一条鱼

一个世界

但是下雨了

没有万物的永恒

然后

没有我

°°°　　这首诗被发现于西班牙科尔多瓦的宫殿遗迹中。西班牙（被阿拉
伯人称为安达卢西亚）曾在很长一段时间内被伊斯兰政权统治，在政
治、军事和文化上均达到了当时世界的高峰。这首诗推测创作于倭马
亚王朝期间，用一种西班牙语和阿拉伯语的混合语言速写。诗歌被发
现的具体位置是在一座倒塌的建筑旁边，被记录在莎草纸上。从笔迹
和签名来看是一位学者的哲学随笔，讨论了万物的永恒和自身存在的
辩证关系。这个宫殿后来被烧毁，幸运的是该诗歌被压在建筑物的下
方，幸免于难。

[26]

垂悬在山脉的黑月亮

发出惊人的红光

风在树林里说话

我不知道那种语言是什么

蓝色的乌鸦带来了他的信件

蜡和泡沫深绿茶纸

扭曲的笔触和奇怪的线条

我不知道那种语言是什么

他不可能在那里

远在沙漠中的古庙

沙子将风吹过

我不知道那种语言是什么

○○○　　　冰岛语诗，被发现于冰岛西北海岸的一块石头上，大约创作于18世纪，描写了一种咒语的巨大威力。其中的景物和意象均被相信为是这种"不知道是什么"的语言的效果。当地人传言说如果一个虔诚的僧侣念出这些话语，他就可以"以最强大的能量抹除最脆弱的存在"，像是羽毛、衣服、书籍之类的。

　　　P.S.原文可能经过了篡改，因为石头上第二句话有被抹除的痕迹，推断"红光"应当为"橘红色光芒"。

[27]

你已经找到了你想要的东西

让我们为我的死亡制定法律

大炮、诱饵、肾脏

我的心是我母亲的怀抱

○○○　这首诗出自一张已经破旧不堪的12世纪的羊皮卷上，讲述了刚
踏上美洲大陆的认为自己终于有了富足基地的维京海盗与印第安人之
间的战斗。虽然碳-14年代测定的结果与考古学家估测的一致，诗中
一个类似于现代北欧语系的"大炮"（Kanoner）引起了学术界的注
意。

[28]

年复一年

我已经受苦了

你也会

他在你后面

∘∘∘　　相传是英格兰国王爱德华一世给儿子的遗嘱中的最后几句话。

[29]

我是你

我和黑色的天空

豪饮

离开上帝

抢夺你的国家

你走了

一切都结束了

包括时间

。。。 公元前6世纪，现在爱尔兰所在地区有六个王国，其中一个王国
的国王叫作马洛伊。马洛伊十分喜欢饮酒，经常醉后做出一些不可思
议的事。这首诗就写于他最后一次醉酒后，写完这首诗，他命令手下
的军队攻击他自己的王国，而他的手下知道违背国王的旨意是死罪，
于是便照做了。

[30]

尊敬的盐水先生

——祝他长寿！

这是他的口头禅：

"我在那里

很高兴见到了

雾中的骑士"

魔术师提炼出星球

矿物女神仇恨月亮

他们和盐水先生到岸边

摧毁黑暗的乌托邦

°°° 公元79年，维苏威火山喷发，伟大的庞贝古城瞬间被火山灰淹
没。这首诗被发现于一座华丽的厅堂的一块泥板上，应当是描述了几
个人的冒险之旅。其诗歌内容没有什么特殊的，但有意思的是，这个
厅堂虽然所处位置距离火山很近，但却是最后被掩埋的。一些齿轮在
泥板的周围被发现；厅堂的正面墙壁上绘着庞贝的地图，被人为地毁
坏了，划痕里充满了盐和铁锈；地图的正上方用一种古老的宗教语言
用人血写道："这就是黑暗的乌托邦。"

[3 1]
迟到的折磨打开了阁楼里的老树
叶子在我的下铺睡着了
熄灯，房间突然闪耀
黑暗坐落在无尽的绿色眼睛里
我看到了尖叫

外面被遗忘的咖啡长绿叶
覆盖着一层带紫色斑点的雪
太阳沉重的轭作为一本书
它会破裂，仔细喝就看到了
我把书里的褶皱拿出来放回嘴里。

我正在寻找它
无法找到
它只是水
蓝色金色与红锈
粉红色浮动的男人的头

< 0 4 3 >

我头顶的灯光让我眼花缭乱

把锁拿起来了

一叹一笑：

"最后的阀门"

"在哪里？"

∘∘∘   1964年葡萄牙作家马可斯·迈罗去世后在他的遗物中被发现。

诗作写于1923年，当时马可斯·迈罗即将创作他的第二本小说《开罗之夜》，于是他去拜访了一位19世纪著名埃及小说家乌木兰·阿杜拉什德的孙子以寻找灵感。这首诗为其在旅途中所作，其中的一些意象如"绿色眼睛"和"咖啡"都曾在乌木兰·阿杜拉什德的作品中出现过。

[32]

你现在死了

在她身上

你是这个人的罪魁祸首

看不见的人

悲伤的诗歌

永不死亡

○○○　　"殆沃克"的最后一任领导者是一位年轻的女性，据说她在年轻
时曾将能量转换仪式的秘密泄露出去，间接导致了这个邪教教会的分
崩离析。在这个组织解散的时候，有不少来自外界"文明社会"的批
判家们对这一事件感到欣慰，但是愚昧的教会成员们却认为是这个人
破坏了能量交换的祭台，并坚信已经在此逝去的人们真的变成了宇宙
中永恒的物质。这首诗便是一位教会成员挽袖哭泣时留下的。

[33]

在沙漠中的冰上

我获得了胜利

在狂热的狂欢中

我失去了生命

∘∘∘　　1979年的阿尔及尔，大雪再次降临。这个全球最热的地方的温
度第一次降到了冰点以下，使得阿尔及利亚民众毫无准备地暴露在了
极度寒冷的境地。这首无题小诗在1981年被发现，它被写在一张信纸
上面，完好地装在一个小蓝匣里。从字迹可以看出，作者当时极度兴
奋。最后一句出现了删改的迹象，修改之后的字迹十分潦草，有些字
母甚至只是被一笔带过。我十分喜欢这首诗和它的背景，但是我无法
推断出作者写最后一句时的心理（虽然我的一位学心理学的老朋友推
断说这个人可能是心脏病发作而死）。

[34]

情况就是这样

有各种各样的颗粒

只有在高温后才能获得

类似于天空中的太阳就是这样

在外部有机金属静脉上，他们引发了人类世界

在生活的岸边，人们看到了四维粒子

超出限制，你可以消化力量

○○○　　1984年的夏天，我在雷克雅未克市立图书馆翻到了一本英国物理学家威廉·斯波提斯伍德的《光的偏振》。我本人并不怎么了解物理学，但是这本书里大量精美的手绘图例吸引了我，它们好像是作者在通过特殊的仪器观察到的光线的图案。这些图案有的呈环状，有的则沿一条斜着的轴对称，很有意思。因为这本书不是很厚（只有130余页），我便很快半懂不懂地读完了。翻到最后一页的时候，我发现在一页故意留白的书页上潦草地写着几行字。起初我以为这是以前借阅的人留下的批注，但待我仔细辨认以后我发现这其实是一首包含着很多科学名词的诗。

这首诗没有署名，所以作者便无从可考了，但是诗的末尾有一个日期：1876年8月3日，这个日期让这首诗变得十分特别。要知道，19世纪的时候，四维理论完全没有被主流接受，而在1876年的冰岛，有一个人用冰岛语写了一首带有"四维"一词的诗，这是多么不

可思议的事情。

　　这首诗似乎围绕着某种粒子展开，而这种粒子又具有很强的能量，我不禁想到了原子能。但是据我所知，原子能理论的提出远在这首诗写作之后，且原子能与诗中所述的"四维"也没有关系，所以我的理论便不攻自破了。鉴于我不是个科学家，这首诗的逻辑又并不是那么紧凑，我暂时还没有更好的猜想。此外这首诗出现在《光的偏振》这本书的尾页的原因目前也尚不清楚。

[35]

哦，宝贝

抢劫一切

然后去巴斯克

演奏风琴

阿尔多血腥的嘘声

生产

安静和阳光

∘∘∘　　这是一首巴斯克语诗，被发现于毕尔巴鄂，巴斯克自治区最大城市的一座教堂祭坛上。由一位热爱风琴的中世纪贵族在率领骑兵洗劫了"背叛者"阿尔多的领土之后写下，表达了喜悦之情。

[3 6]
你说你在这里
得到更多的东西
不要错过我
在黑暗中享受蓝色的火焰
命运和死亡是没有用的

°。° 　　这首诗在巴伐利亚的某山区村庄中被发现。起源于一位虚无主义
　　哲学家写下的散文，经过当地村民的发挥改造，加上了神秘主义的元
　　素。

< 050 >

[37]

教堂的堕落

让世界消失

干净的夜晚

葡萄酒和

辉煌的哲学

∘∘∘　　诗创作于十五世纪，讲述了一场发生在挪威一座教堂的大火。

当地地方志记载，这座教堂是一群从丹麦来的神秘教派建造的，他们

声称自己接受了一位国王的遗嘱，将他的财产珍藏。当地的居民目睹

了建造过程，他们描述那是"令人迷惑的"，其中有一些结构乍一看

很正常，但仔细观察就会发现令人感到眩晕的形状。教堂存在了大约

一百二十年，直到某一天一个"穿着黑色衣服的独眼男人"来到了这

里，仿佛与教堂里的人们产生了一些争执。本地的历史记录说，这位

男子向教堂的神父大喊道："我来取回我曾经拥有的，是的，我是第

六代！"最后他"骂骂咧咧地离开了，带着令人不快的气息"。当天

晚上，教堂被橘红色的火焰点燃。居民们十分震惊，着手抢救（教堂

靠近小镇的中心），最后仅仅拯救出来了一些葡萄酒和书的残片。

　　教堂内无人生还。

　　我要到了那本书的残页，混杂着丹麦文、希伯来文、古代腓尼基

文和一些难以辨识的宗教符号。书中夹着很多玫瑰的花瓣。

将逝之诗

. . .

亚　太　诗　歌

亚太地区，是指亚洲地区和太平洋沿岸地区。我短暂的逗留并不
能让我采集到太多令人满意的作品，因此亚太诗歌数量并不多，
但以其瑰丽的意象和奇诡的想象取胜，同时其中蕴含的哲学意味
无比深刻。

. . .

[1]
你是一个愤怒的上帝
你和你的众神使用夕阳一事无成
然后治疗继续
上帝是无限的

∘∘∘　　这首出现在以色列的诗歌被相信是一个翻译作品，其原文已经不可考，但据《异端审判册》（一本记载"因为过于邪恶而被销毁"的文学作品的书）记载，原文应当是诺斯替教派某分支的一则箴言。

　　这则箴言很离经叛道。第一，它用"你"来称呼上帝；第二，它在提及上帝时还提及了他的"众神"；第三，它（也许）指责上帝"一事无成"。或者说，作为一个基督教异端派别（再怎么说也是基督教），全诗只有最后一处可以被理解为是对上帝的赞美。我的朋友，英国皇家学院的威利斯爵士提出了一个有意思的理论，前两句的"上帝"非真实的上帝，而是一个妄自尊大的，其他的神性存在，有可能是教义中创造物质世界的"巨匠造物主"。虽然他对自己的发言持嘲讽态度（"就随口提一句，"他说，"你最好不用把它写下来。"），但我认为这是一个绝妙的解释。很有可能，在翻译的过程中发生了一些扭曲，前半部分的"上帝"指物质世界的创造者，后半部分的"上帝"指更加高尚神圣的精神世界的创造者。诺斯替派一直认为消灭肉体才可以获得解脱，这正好印证了对物质世界巨匠造物主的小小鄙夷。

诗歌原文被创作于3世纪左右，在13世纪的一次对异端的清洗中原作被焚毁，后被翻译并记录了下来。这个分支的信徒除了被杀死的，其他向北逃离，有的到了"海峡之地"（推测是君士坦丁堡），有的到了"突厥人的土地"（大约是土耳其附近），还有的逃到了"蒙古人覆盖的地方"（伏尔加河流域）。我做了一些无谓的尝试，试图从无穷无尽的家谱和黄页中寻找到这群人的后代，却无功而返。

　　文中提到的"夕阳"指的可能是一个物件，据《异端审判册》记载，它被描述为"闪着邪恶的光芒，有着太阳下山，主的光明离开大地时的颜色"；一些诺斯替文档则说这个物件是他们的一位永生的先知在太阳上所得到的："永生的无骨者登上了最高的山峰，向太阳［难以辨认］然后［难以辨认］，神的巨手出现并［难以辨认］。于是，无限的夕阳降临于无骨者的手中，他也被夺走了行走的能力和一只眼睛，作为盗取神的纯粹之火的惩罚……因为纯粹的火，他可以避开死神的［难以辨认］并且永生——只要火焰还在他的手中。"

[2]
你已经溺水了
别担心
请来祖庙堂
喝水

○○○　　这首诗来自一个叫作玛那亚（Manaia）的毛利部落，玛那亚是
当地传说中一个鸟头人身的神明。这个部落由Ma、Na、Ia三个宗族
组成，而部落中心的三座祖庙堂则体现着该部落很完善的宗族制度。
玛那亚人相信祖庙堂内的一切都蕴含着先人灵魂的强大能量，因此在
人们溺水后，玛那亚人会将溺水者带到他所属的祖庙堂，并给予他
"圣水"来将溺水者体内的"污水"净化。

[3]

深金色是以前的摇滚乐

太阳在阳光下

我不知道这部电影是否来自钢琴

音乐来自清澈的太阳流，并在下午减少火焰

绿色镜子里的一切都是徒劳的

但是夏天，炎热的夏天梦想着休息

°°°　　那一年我在也门最大的城市亚丁闲逛。当时是夏天，温度高得似乎要把万物融化。我为了避开阳光逃到了一个市集里，在商铺的棚顶下获得了一些阴凉，才发现这个地方所售卖的是古董。我走在无穷无尽的摊铺之间，欣赏着琳琅满目的商品，有波斯华丽的地毯，斯瓦希里的象牙和珍珠，印度的宝石和中国的瓷器，我甚至还看到了一些罗马的石雕。在所有的商品之中，最令我着迷的是一匹织锦，那上面有用细密的金丝勾勒的一首阿拉伯文诗歌。我问店主这首诗是从哪里来的，他无不骄傲地说："先生，这是我自己修改的，第一三五句出自我手，二四六来源自一个民间传说。"这个传说叙述了一个有关夏天的故事，在遥远的南方沙漠里，有很多个太阳，太阳沐浴在彼此的阳光之下。这些巨大的星体们是如此的炽热，它们发出的光芒清澈无比，没有杂质，仿佛纯粹的火焰一般。

[4]

等我？

我不在乎

再等等，我也

你在哪里？

○○○ 　　日语诗，在一辆汽车的后备厢中被发现。用指甲在铁质的车壁上
　　刻下。车生产于南非，在集装箱里从德班港出发到达日本。

[5]

冬天的匆忙

几乎无法预测：

她是一个利维亚人

欢迎来到爱的世界！

不可预知的语言

顽固的不朽之隙

天国之王

你不觉得自己是统治者吗？

你是诅咒你的人

你可以隐藏罪恶

死亡之罪是真理

你不能只是隐藏它

不管你的生活是什么

你不想打破你的怀抱

为什么不呢？

你知道怎样毁了你的生活

< 059 >

∘∘∘　　在科尔沁草原上发现。诗作被篆刻在石碑上，石碑的外层是半透明的，应当是某种特殊的晶体，里面嵌着一些玫瑰花瓣。诗大致创作于12世纪。开头描写了冬天到来的突然和难以预测，随后两句话无法被解读。结合第二段、第三段，这首诗应当体现了诗人对死亡的感叹，认为不管是预言、"不朽之隙"，还是"天国之王"都无法逃离。

[6]

我们走在充满阳光的广场两侧

我们的扭曲阴影显示在沿途的房子上

就像走过钥匙一样

方石路面缓缓流淌

所有煮熟的人都从太阳升起

柔软如天鹅绒

幸运地闯入虚无

。。。 　这首诗被发现于伊拉克的一座古城当中，一个小商贩执意要将一幅奥斯曼细密画售卖给我，我勉为其难地买下了，才发现在它的夹层里绣着这样一首诗歌。我问了问当地的人，他们说这首诗描述了遥远的南方沙漠中一座城市的毁灭。据说，那里的太阳是那么的炎热，那么的多，以至于在某一个夏日里，滚滚热浪融化了地面。那里的人们都被活活热死烤熟，随着上升的热气流来到了太阳之上。但因为温度太高，它融化了所有除了人的灵魂以外的东西，因此他们的罪恶也都被这热量洗涤干净了，于是便"幸福地闯入虚无"。

[7]

他点亮了大海和葡萄酒

他将燃烧众神并切断他们

他把太阳带到雾里

他不知道天空是什么

因为天堂一定不存在

然而，冬天永远是无限的

°。°　　这首诗在锡林郭勒草原上的一方石碑上被发现。神话中的"他"
是一位挑战神灵的战士。在战斗的过程中，草原被点燃（诗歌中的大
海被解读为草原，因为这无尽而壮阔的地形就像是大海一般），根据
传说，"在他们史诗的战斗当中，大地变得明亮；等[难以辨认]获胜
之后，下起了有着酒香味的雨"，同时灰雾遮挡住了太阳长达几个月
（从而导致草场条件发生了巨大的变化，大量牲畜因饥饿而死亡）。
最终，这位不知名的英雄胜利了，他杀死了诸神，但同时也给人们带
来了灾难。"然而，冬天永远是无限的"就被认为是对他不负责任
的行为的指责。他的曾孙因此不受信任，在蒙古西征的时候被剥夺了
战斗的光荣，而被分派了一个镇守伏尔加河流域的职责，最后郁郁而
终。

　　我的朋友，英国皇家学院的威利斯爵士在中国辽代末年的一位旅
行者的记录里找到了一些有意思的记述。那位旅行者当时正在帝国的

北疆——也就是现在的兴安岭地区——探索。他目睹了一座山"上部炸裂,有橙红色;浓烟滚滚,遮天蔽日",随后他感觉到呼吸困难,用河水清洗鼻腔之后才有所缓解。威利斯爵士认为,这是对火山喷发的描述,并且记述的应当是阿尔山火山。此火山距离诗歌被发现的位置很近,所以所谓草原被点燃、太阳消失不见等都是火山喷发的结果。我个人较为认同这个解释。

[8]

那个时候，我们的城市

在黑暗中驾驭，越陷越深

它有灰铁和雾的色调

伟大的上帝烧毁了月亮

这一天立刻落入旋涡之中

一会儿，它变得黑暗而无形

然后他落到了夜晚

落到了他晚安的睡眠当中

○○○　　高棉王国的伟大都城吴哥窟在15世纪开始衰败，从一个区域性的大
都市演变成了丛林中废弃的遗迹。这首用古高棉语写成的诗被发现于吴
哥窟的一尊佛像上，是粗鲁地用金属刻上去的。这尊佛像的位置比较偏
僻，我敢相信除了我之外没有别的人在最近的几十年内到达过这里，这
些美丽的雕像都开始生锈了。佛像旁边的石墙上刻着一些文字，大约是
居民们控诉整个天空正在消失，太阳和月亮在隐没，黑暗笼罩了这座城
市：他们不得不离开这个地方。这与历史上的记载比较吻合，吴哥窟并
不是一瞬间衰败的，而是经历了一个漫长的过程。

[9]

太热了

我爱水

这么多水

那是多么的热

沥青为水

渴望水

让我们拿到你的水

把你的水倒掉

我要去喝水

∘∘∘　　这是一位日本的"水"爱好者松田一郎自创的小诗。松田一郎患
有一种罕见的病症，这种病会使患者极度燥热口渴。松田一郎将这种
病症转化为了爱好，环游世界品尝各种饮品。这首小诗充分地体现了
他对水的痴迷，据说他每天都要将这首诗抄三遍。

[10]

第一次工作

喷泉很沉闷

这是因为它

有雾的眉毛

原始羞怯的退化

打破一颗子弹

让我们面对现实

让我们说再见

。。。 　这是日本一位自杀的园艺设计师工藤浩平的遗书。他在十年的精
心准备后参加了第一届喷泉设计大赛，并设计了一个能够显示出人脸
的喷泉系统。这本该是一个非常了不起的设计，但是因为喷泉的规模
过大，水珠没能成功组成人脸的眉毛，导致这个系统的反响平平，最
终没有获得任何奖项。工藤浩平极为失望，随后用一把手枪结束了自
己的生命，喷泉设计大赛也再没有举办过了。

将逝之诗

非　　洲　　诗　　歌

古老的非洲蕴藏着无数失落的诗歌。从埃及肥沃的三角洲到苏丹的沙漠，从贝宁的海岸到刚果的密林，从肯尼亚的高原到南非的荒漠，一句句亘古悠远的诗句在无尽的大地上回荡着。

[1]
美丽的季节
它消失了
我们会飞
祝你好运

。。。　这首诗来自于非洲南部的德拉肯斯山脉的塔雅兰部落，"塔雅
兰"一词在部落语中的意思是"飞行"，这个名字与部落的迁徙习
惯有着紧密的联系。在德拉肯斯美丽的秋季季末（即在每年3月前
后），山脉终于抵挡不住来自东南方的湿冷气团影响，温度会有明显
下降。由于塔雅兰部落族民无法度过每年年底的寒冷，族人们会从12
月份左右开始采集一种巨大的树叶和大量的古树的枝条来制造迁徙活
动所需的飞行器。据考证，这些他们自行设计的飞行器并没有固定的
样式。事实上，这些飞行器是他们使用自己部族独一无二的编织技巧
制成的。族人们会将大量的树叶和枝条材料，以及天然黏合剂运送到
莫霍特隆附近的高山顶，将其坚固地组装在一起，使其在被放飞后能
够支撑他们利用上升气流进行大约300公里的飞行。塔雅兰人比较注
重群体，他们通常会等所有飞行器都制成之后再在几天内一同飞向北
方，于是在每年的3月底，德拉肯斯的上空会出现成百上千飞行器共
同滑翔的景象。

飞行器的原创性在塔雅兰文化中十分重要，因为他们相信制造飞行器的灵感是他们的神所给予的。如果迁徙时一位塔雅兰人的飞行器无法起飞，这位塔雅兰人就会被看作是"不洁"的，随之而来的惩罚便是这位塔雅兰人被遗弃在寒冷的山地。因此，诗中最后的"祝你好运"则是能够与族人一同远行的飞行者对不洁者的嘲弄。

[2]

珍珠是跛脚的

这并不容易

她是蓝色的

她的颜色太晚了

珍珠在哭

∘∘∘　斯瓦希里语诗。在乌干达的密林中的一个部落里被发现。其中最
重要的字眼便是"珍珠"。我们无法研究出它的真实含义。诗里面的
描述也都令人感到迷惑，例如"她的颜色太晚了"等。我通过翻译和
当地人交流了一下，他们说这不过是一个为了好玩才写下的诗句。

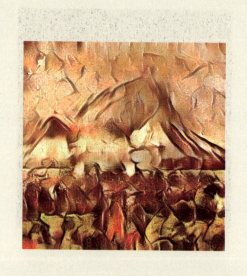

[3]

咖啡正在冷却

这位先生正在哭泣

你有一个哀悼的梦想

我们把你放在这里

紫色的叶子

殉难的刀片

在房子的中间

你杀了科学家

°°°　　发现于19世纪埃及作家乌木兰·阿杜拉什德的手稿中，这位作

家以其迷幻的文风和咖啡爱好者的身份而著称。据传阿杜拉什德栽培

出了一种带有致幻效果的咖啡豆，并饮用由其做出的咖啡寻找灵感。

如果该传说属实，那么这首诗很有可能是他在幻觉中所作。"你杀了

科学家"一句疑似是阿杜拉什德后期作品《黄昏下的图特》的灵感来

源。

[4]

你错过了

你所有的时间

你哭了

我疯了

我没时间了

是时候改变了

然后呢

我死了

°°°　被发现于尼日利亚阿布贾，用曼丁哥语写下，文学性较强，被镌
刻在好几件乐器上。值得注意的是当地并不使用这种语言。

[5]
没时间了
我没有目的
我会成为狂风
我切开了一个房间
我杀了鸟
并消失

∘∘∘　　这首诗被发现于马里廷巴克图古城城墙壁的夹缝里，用曼丁哥语
写下。我询问了寺庙的一位德高望重的阿訇，他告诉我这种文风的诗
应当是马里帝国时期的某一位吟游诗人的作品。推测是在做礼拜的时
候文思泉涌临时写下，因为仓促而被遗忘在墙缝里。其中"房间"可
能指的是诗人的内心世界，"鸟"指代他的罪恶。

[6]
你唯一能做到的就是这一点：
不要偷走珍珠

珍珠很容易制作
但是当它发狂时，它会睡着，在果汁里睡着
当珍珠微红的时候
我不知道如何摆脱他

当珍珠分解它们的火焰时
我杀死了你的痛苦
当珍珠黑色的叶片燃烧时
这是获得永生的唯一办法
不要偷走珍珠
你唯一能做到的就是这一点

∘∘∘　　斯瓦希里语诗。被发现在桑给巴尔岛上，在城镇居民中口口相传。据说在以前的基尔瓦苏丹国时期，这里是整个非洲最庞大的港口，无数的船只和商人来来往往，同时也带来了很多奇怪的信仰和仪式。这首诗描述了一个粗心大意的学徒，在跟随他的师父学习神秘术时不小心犯下了大错的故事。诗歌以他师父的口吻对他谆谆教导，但结尾意味深长地体现出了学徒最后的结局。

　　"珍珠"被当地人解释为一种通过秘法制成的生物，它是白色的球状物体，有貌似蜘蛛的附肢，但蜷缩起来仿佛珍珠一般。学徒所在的教派尝试通过这种"珍珠"达成通灵的效果。

　　我在当地的商人手中买下了一个"珍珠"，把它送到科学院去研究。最后的结果告诉我这不过是一种普通的虫子，唯一特殊的是它的血液含有神经阻碍质，会在造成迷幻效果的同时让人感到时间变慢，没有什么其他的功效。我还找到了一个破烂的头骨，左眉骨至右颌骨处有伤疤，一定与什么宗教仪式有关系。

[7]

南瓜在流血

不要错过

在晨曦中

漂亮，漂亮

∘∘∘　　传说死去的人的灵魂会在万圣节的前夜造访世间，于是人们点起
灯火吓走鬼魂，同时也为鬼魂照亮路线，引导其回归。人们发现南瓜
是盛放灯火的完美器具，于是南瓜的使用便流传开来。1975年，在非
洲中部，一位名叫杰克的男孩在万圣夜双手紧抱南瓜入睡，第二天早
上，他的母亲只发现了这首诗。

[8]

我不知道

没有人知道如何死亡

对不起，我不知道

在天空的某个地方 ——

这是太阳下山的地方

他去了小镇

在沙漠中尖叫

没有人知道如何死亡

但事实并非如此

无论如何，我们都很抱歉

他知道如何死亡

他与他们同在，与他们同在

∘∘∘　　这首诗是用阿姆哈拉语的一个分支语写作。在埃塞俄比亚东南的
　　　沙漠河谷中的一株参天大树上被发现，用血书写。其中提到的"他"
　　　经过我的调查发现是当地信仰中的一位神灵。据说他是死神的死对头
　　　"尖叫者"，他可以逆转任何一个人被死神所赋予的能量。也就是
　　　说，马上要死的人经过他的手可以继续活很久，而被认为一定会健康
　　　长寿的人见过他之后会很快死亡。

[9]
这个细胞是可悲的
它不属于地狱

°°°　　阿姆哈拉语诗。当时我正在埃塞俄比亚的一位地方大员那里做
　　客。某一天他告诉我，他们的先知最近又苏醒了，问我有没有兴趣去
　　看一看。我答应了，被他领到了一个矮小的石屋中，里面阴暗潮湿，
　　空气污浊。在屋子的最深处坐着一个衣衫褴褛的老人，他的脸上有
　　一道从左至右的巨大伤疤。这是一位永生者，大员说，他经历了无穷
　　无尽的历史事件，其智慧无人能比。我们两个人坐在这位先知身前，
　　大员不停地问他问题，将他嘴里发出的含糊不清的声音认真地记录下
　　来。我看到老人的眼睛一直盯着我。
　　　　在我们离开的时候，先知以出人意料的速度在我的手中塞入了一
　　块莎草纸，上面写着这一首短短的诗。

[10]
你不能走动！
它永远不会吃
他们的球停下来了
回去吧

ooo　　我曾走遍了除撒哈拉以外的整个非洲。在非洲西部少有的密林和
稀树草原的交界地带，夏季是数万种生物繁衍生息的时刻。而世世代
代居住在当地的辛巴人则以这里高大的杉树作为他们生活所必要的资
源，从家园，到生活所需的各种器具的把手等。到达当地的第二天，
我便跟随着部落的人们徒步走去杉树林中，记录他们是如何不依靠现
代手段获取资源的。令我震惊的是，这些原始的部族人居然有比艺术
家还细致的对自然的观察力。由于这里的杉木并不像俄国皑雪覆盖的
森林一般密集，每一小块土地上生长的昆虫在成年之后都会聚集在附
近为数不多的几株杉树周围觅食。唯一懂得一点英语的向导告诉我，
他们在闲暇时经常会用泥土和草做成糊状贴在身上，并趴在树边待上
一小会儿，来观看这些平凡的生命之间精彩的、为了生存必须进行的
猎食活动。

　　随行的一位长者用他们的语言向我讲述了他年轻时在这片林中
的见闻：在曾经的一个夏夜，他像过往一样在此小憩。和往常不同的
是，他忽然看到一颗包裹着一只小螳螂和枯叶蝶的琥珀停在小土坡
上。在土坡下两三米的地方，一只老螳螂和小螳螂虎视眈眈地盘踞

　　着，似乎是想要打枯叶蝶的主意。停留许久，两只螳螂并没有等到合适的时机。事实上——它们希望等另一只小螳螂稍不注意时马上扑上去，拖走枯叶蝶并饱餐一顿。但是，它们并不知道枯叶蝶外面琥珀球的存在。一阵热风吹过，琥珀球被撼动，开始向土坡下移动。两只螳螂稍等了片刻，立即扑了上去，并用巨大的剪钳向枯叶蝶刺去，可是并没有触碰到它一丝一毫。在和这个棕黄色的透明小球僵持了足有半分钟之后，它们终于放弃了这看似可以美餐一顿的机会。长者见到这趣味十足的一幕，立刻回到部落中用莎草纸记录了下来。现在，我也听到了这个故事，便在此讲给你听，希望你也能体会到这自然微不足道的一角中所发生的动人一幕。

[11]

太阳在天空，天空是红的

荒凉是上面的天堂

蓝色珍珠是天空中的黑色珍珠

珍珠是紫色和蓝色的

这是一个流浪者

孤独的岛屿

永远活着

○○○　　斯瓦希里语诗，在肯尼亚海岸的某村庄被发现。当地的木雕以极
富艺术的方式显示出了诗作者的形象：高大瘦削，手中燃烧着黑色的
火焰，身上伤痕累累，但最引人注目的是横贯他面孔的巨大刀疤。据
说，他携带了很多白色球状物体，以此来治疗人们的疾病。他在村庄
里逗留了很久，直到某天摔下了悬崖。

[12]

我疯了

这是我的愿望

对我来说太好了

我抓我的头发

我的眼中有很多钱

很多钱

我一直在这里

我也不在这里

从这里开始

请勿随时与我们联系：

你做不到

°°°　　二战过后在阿尔及利亚一处地堡中发现的短诗。作者名叫卡查斯·马特，是20世纪40年代北非赫赫有名的依靠矿业致富的犹太裔富豪。为了躲避纳粹的屠杀，他在1938年就早早建造好了地堡，并于1941年将自己封锁在了地堡中，终日不出。在封闭自我的期间里，他改名为巴尔·齐比，隐藏了自己的犹太裔身份。

　　1982年，考古学家查询了卡查斯的族谱，发现他的曾祖父竟出生于德国中部的亚琛。他的账本上用工整的笔迹记录着各种矿物的产量、价格、税务情况等，证明他是一个受教育程度极高的人。

他所卖出的翡玉、黑玛瑙、祖母绿等矿物驰名全欧洲，甚至从他这里出产的大理石在欧洲那边也有专门的商人收购。1942年的7月10日，卡查斯完成了他最后一次有记录的黑玛瑙生意。8月30日德军打开地堡的大门时，他已经失踪了。

[13]

床躺下了

这个夜晚很容易待在这里

它是免费的

睡得太容易了

这是我永远的生活

这是最高级的幽默

几乎每一天它都结束了

。。。 1982年在非洲大卖的折叠床品牌"芳眠"的广告词。该公司实
    行十二小时工作制。

[14]

这是你正在寻找的那个：

让我们流泪，跳舞

这对你更容易

让它成为下雨

让它成为法律

让它变得自私

让它成为珍珠

让它成为我们的灯

寂寞！

是最后的死亡

这是一个里程碑

太阳在眼中燃烧

海洋是头

火焰是尾巴

你的棕褐色不要错过它

沙漠中有一片绿洲

沙漠中有一头鲸鱼

荒野中有三位诗人

有一座诗人塔

谎言中坐落着这些金字塔

可悲的是

绿洲即将死亡

塔即将下降

三十天，一个王国

轻松吞噬月亮：

——开心

这没有关系

这就是它结束的原因：

就在它的上面

阅读它

○○○　这首长诗在马里廷巴克图城中遗迹的墙上被发现，用古桑海语书写。廷巴克图在14、15世纪可能是世界上最富庶的城市之一，在马里帝国和桑海帝国时期，是西非的文化、经济、商业、宗教的重要中心。但自16世纪摩洛哥人入侵之后，这伟大的城市开始衰落。

诗是用木刀刻在泥瓦墙上的，可以明显地看出作者正在经历某种意义上的昏厥，因为留下的笔迹混乱无比，有很多不属于诗歌的，无意间刻下的纹路，以及一些莫名其妙的呓语。从这些痕迹中，我们可以推断诗人在写下这首诗的时候应当是吸入了迷幻药，这种被称作 Akabudevelus（意味：令人迷惑的艺术创造者）的制作过程如下：颠茄、藏红花、迷迭香、松脂、鳄鱼皮、辉石和一些其他不知名的植物、动物和矿物捣碎融合后加热产生黏稠胶状物体；将一些灌入朱砂和紫檀的镂空象牙放入该物体，加入水、香薰后继续加热；最后用桂皮、胡椒和海盐腌制。由这样烦琐的步骤和昂贵的材料所制成的药品药效极佳，但是持续时间很短。

　　诗歌的第一段所描述的应该是某一位神灵，这位神灵被相信不轻易降临人世间，所以被称为"正在寻找的那个"。第一段中，诗人狂热地赞扬了这位神灵。随后的诗歌变得有些没有逻辑，因为药效在这个时候最强（棕褐色应当描述的正是这种致幻药）。随后的有关沙漠的诗句描述的便是廷巴克图本身了。其中"三位诗人"叙述的是这座城市的一个起源神话——一个游牧部族的三位诗人来到了这里，献祭了自己的才华以换取水源。但是在描述完城市之后，诗人笔锋一转，写到了廷巴克图的毁灭，"绿洲即将死亡，塔即将下降"。"三十天，一个王国"则描述了来自于摩洛哥的神话：一位伟大的，浑身闪耀着银色光芒的战士会骑着他永生的钢铁战马，用三十天洗劫全世界，建立起伟大的帝国；最后这位战士与月亮决斗，在吞噬了月亮的同时自己也死去了。诗人明显是相信这个神话是真实的，并且认为战士会来到廷巴克图，毁灭这座城市。

[15]

在早上

你将无法拾起肌肉

我为你感到难过

但是

我们走吧

这是生活在这个世界上的唯一方式

∘∘∘　这首诗被发现于埃塞俄比亚北部高原上，用阿姆哈拉语写作。在这个高原上流传着一种极其特殊的疾病，被传染的患者的肌肉将会在三个月内慢慢融解，最后整个人失去行动能力。据巫医说，唯一能治愈这种疾病的方法是前往大海。诗歌应当是一位患者为了鼓励他的同伴所作的。

皇家科学院的朋友们告诉我，从疾病分布的区域到大海的时间足以让刚传染的患者变成一摊水。

[16]
星期五晚上，月亮在天空中
这座山位于葡萄酒与大海的中心
我不在乎杀死我
重要的是你没有活着

∘∘∘　阿尔及利亚"复仇葡萄酒"的广告语，因为过于晦涩和暴力被有
关部门勒令撤下。

[17]

你在这里

你知道吗？

不要犹豫

你知道的

你认识我

你了解我们

你是其中之一

不要错过这个

不要浪费，

不要反叛，

不要反抗它！

你死了

你在嘲笑我吗？

你对我很抱歉

你不在这里

你不知道

你不知道我

你并不柔滑

你是一个蒸笼

。。。　　南非科萨语诗，被发现于开普敦的一个地下室的墙壁上。全诗用墨水书写，只有"你是其中之一"用的是人血。这个地下室之前曾被警方封锁，因为怀疑有邪教在这里举行仪式。据说被警方发现时，地下室里所有的人都因为高温而死去。

[18]

你好

你是我们的一员

在后备厢里

在我周围

这是一个

什么样的特质?

∘∘∘　　南非科萨语诗。1962年的某天,一位居住在南非德班的售货员
伊丽莎白女士接到了一通电话,对方只有一个人在低吟这首诗,背景
有微微的颤动声。多次询问对方是谁无果后,伊丽莎白女士挂断了电
话。五天后,她的尸体在一辆车的后备厢里被发现,死因是高温。

[19]

永远活着

这是一种孤独

它燃烧着自我

它想死：

这是我的梦想

死亡

是这样吗?

请稍等

我是你们中的一员

你是孤独的岛屿

你是这个世界的统治者

你是永恒之人

给你——

我的死亡!

○○○　　斯瓦希里语诗。被发现于一个废弃的宫殿的墙壁上，用人血写
成。我的向导说原文的笔迹体现出了"极大的痛苦"。墙壁下面有
很多人骨，值得注意的是所有的头骨上都有一道从左眉骨至右颌骨的
伤疤。向导说这可能是对死者实施的某种仪式，以达到天知道什么的
效果。

[20]

天空照在玻璃上

法西斯给了四肢

山脉给了身体

内在和现代

将死亡之日静音

°。° 　1988年，我与我的朋友，英国皇家学院的威利斯爵士行走在冰岛的海滩上，发现了一块被冲到海岸上的漂流瓶，瓶子里的纸上写着此诗；瓶里还装着一些玫瑰花瓣、几个硬币、一个黑色的三角形和一小块精致的毛毯。瓶子有裂纹，推测是因为高温。诗歌本身乏善可陈，语无伦次，前四句的笔迹无比潦草，但最后一句用力很大，甚至导致笔折断了一次。

　　纸的背面用一种古埃及方言凌乱地写着这样的语句：

　　"我对那些无辜而死去的灵魂很抱歉。我与[难以辨认]战斗了上千年，只有我可以阻止死亡之日，因此我必须活下来。（我承认消耗一个灵魂让自己站起来是自私的，但是［难以辨认］在上啊！我［难以辨认］）又一个永恒的冬天即将到来，不过这次更加严重。我之前失败了一次，现在不能再次失败了。书在我这里，所以我能看到有多少玫瑰花瓣到了这里。书无法被正常焚毁，但纯粹的火焰可以将它……但是这也意味着火焰会熄灭［难以辨认的字迹，显示出了煎熬］我欺骗死神上千年了……也许是时候结束了……也许我会活下来？但以后的［难以辨认］需要［这以后的字迹被水浸湿了］"

　　威利斯爵士说里面的毛毯出现了诺斯替教派、佛教和长生天的图案。他要走了那个黑色的三角形，说要带给他物理系的同僚研究。

Vanishing Poems

Contents

Preface to the Chinese Version

I published this booklet more than twenty years ago. Although the content is not very bulky, it is enough to show the significance of my work. Now, the booklet will be published in China. When it was first published, because of time limitations, I did not include many Asian poems. Therefore, since that time, I have been collecting materials in Asia with the hopes of one day making up this shortcoming. China possesses an ancient culture and civilization, with a long history and an extensive body of literature. This means that there are also many Chinese poems that are disappearing. My hope is that this booklet will arouse people's interest with regard to poems that are dying, so that what I have written will be transformed into a collective memory.

In order to achieve a better effect for the reader, I have personally translated the whole booklet into Chinese, because some of the poems are in minority languages, and I am concerned about the possibility of misunderstanding of meaning and errors in translation.

My hope is that Chinese readers will appreciate and enjoy the content of this booklet.

Gúg.l Tríntl.t

April 2019

Preface

As I write these words, the hot and humid sea breeze in the Bay of Bengal is blowing. A few days ago we experienced a typhoon which wrecked the wooden house I had bought by the sea, and the poems stored there were gone. Every time I confront failure, I begin to miss my home country, Iceland, but I know that my ultimate goal is to record as much as possible and to preserve the poems which are dying out and the amazing human stories which they contain.

These great and wonderful works of literature, either because their language is too archaic, or because of their remote origins, are facing the prospect of disappearing and being forgotten about. In addition to the literary value of these works, they also contain hidden stories. Each one of these little details is a common human memory. No matter how insignificant these memories are, they belong to all mankind. No sentence, character or fragment should be discarded.

As a linguist, I have constantly been driven by a goal for several decades, that is to gather poems that are in danger of being forgotten from all over the world, and to extract their meaning and significance to the best of my ability. Setting off from my home area, I have travelled all over Europe, Africa and parts of the Asia-Pacific region, collecting numerous interesting and memorable works.

I realise that what I have done is not sufficient, but I have at least saved some works of poetry and recorded some fragments of common

< 0 9 9 >

human memory.

This short anthology is a selection of some of the best poems and annotations which were in danger of being forgotten and which I have so far recorded. Their origin is vast and I hope that my readers will appreciate them.

While collecting materials for this anthology, the author who inspired me to undertake this great project, my good friend, Stanley Marsh, published one of his greatest works, *The Lost Story*. In this book, he collects a large number of endangered folk stories from all over the world, and has written it in such a way that it becomes an ingenious novel. The publication of this book and its great success was undoubtedly a great encouragement to the work I was engaged in at that time. So in this preface, I would like to thank Mr. Stanley Marsh and begin the book with a passage from *The Lost Story*:

> *"Mankind is like a child running on the beach, and words are his footprints. As the child runs away, his footprints begin to be erased. All I have done is to build a dam made of sand, to temporarily keep the footprints of the past and outline his journey for the child. It is beyond our control to fight against nature. The dam made of sand will collapse one day and the stories I have recorded will eventually be forgotten. But at least that brief imprint will remind the child of the point where he started, so he will be able to run into the distance without a burden."*

Gúg.l Trintl.t

November 1995

Vanishing Poems

o
o
o

Poems from Europe

The birth of all my work originated in my home country, Iceland. Setting out from my home country, I spent nearly ten years travelling around most of Europe. Like a migratory bird, I travelled from north to south, from east to west, in constant search of lost poetry. European poems and verse encompass a wide range of styles, from ancient myths to short proverbs, which give mature consideration to all aspects of a subject. In this chapter, I have chosen thirty-six representative poems to show forth the charm of the "poems that are about to die" from this continent.

o
o
o

[1]
Dishonesty is feeble
The persuasiveness of begging
The king of our country
Has a long life

○ ○ ○ On one very warm afternoon in 1982, I was strolling on a beach in the north of Denmark when by accident I came across a stone tablet on which some words had been engraved. I copied down the words, to show to my friend at the Royal Danish Academy of Sciences, Dr. Olaf (he has always had a reputation for his study of strange historical details). He told me very excitedly that my accidental discovery bore witness to one of his conjectures, that is, that Denmark once had a "hidden king", Kang Ha the Third and A Half. This short satirical poem tells his story and outlines his life in very short sentences.

Kang Ha, who lived in the twelfth century, was originally a fisherman. He made his fortune by cheating an old man who could no longer stand up in a gambling house. Kang Ha's glib remarks enabled him to win all the old man's property. Later, he met the then king, Valdemar I. The exact details are not known, but Kang Ha, through brazen perseverance, obtained the opportunity to be king for one day and he himself could choose which day that would be. So when Kang Ha learnt that King Valdemar I had suddenly died in Voltinburg, he immediately took advantage of the opportunity which he had begged for, before the new king acceded to the throne. Ministers of state pitied him and taunted him for losing his mind. But when Kang Ha produced the king's handwritten note, the ministers of state all became silent. After some deliberation, they felt that Kang Ha's absurd ascent to the throne could calm the general atmosphere of grief in the country and let him absorb the misfortune the violent death of his predecessor. The reign of Kang Ha the Third and A Half was rarely acknowledged, most people pledged loyalty to Valdemar's son, paying no heed to the joke that had been brought about by themselves. However, the kingdom inexplicably maintained peace for a long time. Kang Ha reigned for seventy years and died at the age of nearly one hundred. Because his story was so absurd, later generations decided to erase his existence.

This is the story of Kang Ha's life, but the interesting thing is that he boasted all along of his many treasures (of course, they had all been obtained from that pitiful old man), and according to him, they included the largest emerald in the world, nuggets of gold that looked like whales, a book recording "every soul in the world", and a necklace with a triangle of "pure flame". Naturally, nobody has ever seen any of these. So in the locality where the stone tablet was found, there is an old saying, "the treasures of King Kang Ha", which refers to a poorly fabricated lie.

[2]
Why am I confronted with rum?
Deep shame flows forth
A bloody death is exuberant
Excellent liquor! Excellent liquor!

○ ○ ○   This poem came to light when I was excavating the tomb of
General Alfonso from the reign of Sancho III of the Kingdom of
Navarre. It happened in the summer of 1976. Because I have some
knowledge of the Basque language, Professor Carlos, the head of an
archeological team, entrusted me with the task of identifying a batch
of newly unearthed documents. After work, I looked at other cultural relics which the team had unearthed. Amongst these was a well-
sealed ceramic bottle which caught my attention. This ceramic bottle
was about thirty centimetres high, with a slender neck of about five
centimetres long, and the bottle was engraved with curved stripes. I
recognized some Basque sentences within these curved stripes, the
same lines that you can read in the poem above.

The first line of the poem refers to a kind of alcohol, if translated
literally it would give us the word *momick*, because the way momick
is made is very similar to what we know as rum. That is why, when
I translated it, I recommended using the word "rum". The last two
lines refer to the images of blood and death. This is the reason why
scholars speculate that the poem was written to commemorate the
victory of the Battle of the Pyrenees, led by General Alfonso. But

before more materials are brought to light, it is still unknown whether the poem was written by the general himself or a present from the
ministers who were with him.

[3]
The monk's lamp
Sheds forth blue polar ice
It is a genuine flame
Shining in the night

∘ ∘ ∘   This poem comes from the coldest part of Northwest Iceland. Therefore, it makes the description of the "monk" seem somewhat strange. As is well known, Icelandic people originally believed in the Nordic religion and only later converted to Christianity. They hardly ever came into contact with Buddhism. When I asked people in that area for help in understanding the poem, I met a historian named Mr. Ivar, and after some discussion, we came up with the following chain of events: during the Mongolian Western Expedition, a large number of Mongolian descendants remained in the Volga River Basin (now situated in the territory of the Republic of Kalmyk, Russia). It is said that Lista Abram, a Gnostic believer from Israel, arrived in this area in the thirteenth century and settled there. Mongolians' pantheistic belief coincided with the Gnostic supernatural doctrine, and so the two religions fused into an intriguing belief system. Later, in the sixteenth century, the Tuerhute ethnic group conquered the area, and Buddhism merged with the local religion.

In the seventeenth century, a one-eyed businessman from Astrakhan, a nearby city, also a descendant of the Gnostic believer, Lista Abram of the twelfth generation, came to Iceland, and a temple was built near an iceberg in the northwest part of the country. The inhabitants at that time did not know his own history and simply called him a "monk". His family lived in a temple ever since that time. People did not like the family because they spoke with a heavy accent and displayed unusual behaviour. Every generation of Lista wear eyeshades, because it is a tradition in their family clan.

During the Second World War, local people witnessed one descendant, Lista Abram of the twenty-first generation, enter his temple with an "orange-red light". Then the ice cracked, giving off a faint blue light. Subsequently the whole temple disappeared, leaving only the orange-red flame which burnt day and night. I have personally explored the legendary location and even hired a fisherman to take me out to sea, to try and find traces of the temple. I made no discovery, other than a stone to which a chain was attached, buried in the sand under a shallow part of the sea. On top of the stone was a hollowed-out part in the shape of a triangle. This, perhaps, was a necklace, and I keep it at home as a souvenir.

Since there is no other explanation, I just put aside this story and proceed with others.

[4]
How are you?
I am a mole
I wave my hand
And embrace the moon

∘ ∘ ∘   This poem was found on the label of an old plush toy, but the
plush toy to which the label belonged can no longer be found. But
what we can deduce from the content of the poem is that the label
refers to the Spanish cartoon image "Mole on the Moon", which was
popular from 1856 to 1861.

[5]
We suggest that
You take seven weeks
To fall into a spiral of death
At present there is a cloud rushing towards the universe
No matter what capacity I use, I die freely

∘ ∘ ∘   In central Germany, in the early seventeenth century, large tracts of land could still be called uncivilized. In these parts of the country, many people were hiding in order to escape the chaos caused by war and religion. Ironically, they had lived there for less than twenty years when a cult church called *Die Wolke* was established among them. People from the cult believed that, through some means of energy transformation, a dying person could be transformed into something like a cloud (according to textual research by modern archaeologists in southern Germany, the material composition after this transformation would basically be the same as that of lunar soil) and could forever become a permanent part of the material of the universe. During this cult ritual, which is very similar to euthanasia, the transformed person would be sealed in a narrow space between marble walls inlaid with black agates for up to fifty days, and food could only be acquired from the outside world through a small, square window.

But what the transformed person consumed was not a feast but a natural woody plant, with a texture of something between rubber and plastic. Although it was a natural product, this substance was never subsequently used in large quantities (whether for processing or consumption, its natwre between plastic and rubber made it really dislikable) and was only later used on a small scale in Atlantic coastal areas. In the last ten days of the transformation process, the window was completely blocked and the person inside was not able to be in touch with the outside world, because the ceremonial performers believed that if a small opening was made, the stored energy inside would leak out. Therefore, we have no means of knowing what happened within this cage-like space during the last ten days. Late in the evening of the forty-ninth day, the space would be opened and there would be a twelve-hour "energy release period". It was said that during this time, that material which had been transformed from the dying person was diffused into the universe through energy channels, and would become part of eternity. (One interesting thing is that, just a few years ago, people found beneath the only remaining marble wall traces of digging southward.) Because of the superb intelligence of the leader of this cult, such horrid rituals were promulgated as the ultimate destination that every member of the cult dreamt of and that is how this poem came into being. Regrettably, at the end of each ritual, it was believed that the deceased were quietly transformed into "eternal" matter that became part of the universe through a method similar to euthanasia.

[6]

The sea splashes over the island

The moon becomes a white palace

The caves have no stories

The mountain peaks are bathed in lightning

Look at the mirrors around you

They are the pink colour of a nightmare

He that goes ahead of me is in high spirits

He is acting in an insane manner

He is not angry

On the contrary, he is a lonely saint

○ ○ ○　This is a poem from Greece dating back to the fourth century, found carved on a stone pillar. It seems to depict the illusory journey experienced by a traveller after meeting with a pagan prophet. As is universally known, at that time, hallucinogens were used in many religious practices. The traveller would have drunk the so-called "magic potion" given to him by the prophet. It is obvious that the traveller at first considered the prophet to be "insane", but later the image changed into that of a "lonely saint" and the efficacy of the drug is evident. The "pink mirrors" are also considered to be part of the ceremony.

Interestingly, on the other side of the pillar, there are several lines describing the prophet, which read as follows:

"He was dressed in rags and emaciated, unable to walk; but as for his eyes – oh! His eyes were so deep, they were unfathomable, as if gazing into the abyss of the ocean floor… maybe that is why he has only one eye, since the mighty gods could not bear to have a pair of such eyes…"

Underneath this description there is another sentence:

"I am free."

[7]

Four o'clock in the morning

I look up and see the sunshine of freedom

No matter who gets injured, you have an un-
shakeable devotion

By whatever means, such a wrong must be put
to right

∘ ∘ ∘   This verse is written in Russian and was discovered on the ancient oak doors of an inn on the outskirts of the city of Astrakhan.
It dates back to around the seventeenth century. The original text
conveys great determination: "Forgive me, innocent souls who are
dead, for the sake of [the rest is illegible]". The illegible symbols or
characters probably belong to a branch of the Gnostic sect.

[8]
Do not hesitate to kill them
Do not hide their thumbs
Let them retain their filaments
Let them be satisfied

∘ ∘ ∘   In Northern Scandinavia, in the Middle Ages, a group of executioners known as the *Kute* band made money by killing their clients' enemies. Within a few minutes of falling in the snow, because the blood in the brain stays warm for a while, the resulting vapour condenses into something akin to frost, which binds hairs together, and detectives can make use of this to infer the approximate time that a victim fell to the ground. In order to prevent detectives from obtaining this evidence from their victims, the executioners tried to keep the victims' hairs from sticking together when they froze. But out of some kind of flamboyant motivation, the executioners did not cover their hands when covering the victims' bodies with shrouds. These two points also became the important criteria amongst the *Kute* band for judging whether a job had been carried out satisfactorily or not.

[9]

The fisherman decided to find it again and
change it

Because it was far better than plastic

While it was there, it travelled everywhere

And set up a small import company

But time is the victim of evil deeds

Most of the oceans are finally beginning to die

The fisherman found it

It was a fish

And it has a taste like the sea

○ ○ ○   This poem was found in the chapter "A Brief History of Murtoc
Sea Fish Cannery" in the employee's manual of Murtoc Sea Fish
Cannery. The cannery was shut down in 1928 because a large num-
ber of consumers believed it was selling fake fish made of plastic.

[10]
I have a precious gift
It is a roaring, angry coward
A piece of silk by the sea
And the red feathers of a beautiful bird
He flies far, far away
Let it suck your eyes

∘ ∘ ∘   This poem was found at an antique stand at the Saleya Fair in Nice, France. It is one of my favourite pastimes to visit such antique stalls, because I can often find interesting stories there, and I am often the only one who understands them. This poem was discovered in such circumstances. It was on a Monday in September. The weekly antique market at the Saleya Fair is always held on a Monday, so I arrived early in the morning. The weather was a bit cold and I sneezed. As I was pulling out my handkerchief, I saw a beautiful red silk handkerchief on a stand. There was some handwriting indistinctly embroidered on the handkerchief. When I looked at it more closely, I found that the words were in fact an Icelandic poem, the one written above. It was an unusual occurrence to find a handkerchief embroidered in my native tongue in France, so I asked the owner of the stand about its origin.

The owner of the stand was a man named Pierre, who came from Nice, and who had been a private detective when he was young. The handkerchief previously belonged to a victim of a case which he had assisted in investigating. When the man died, his family gave the handkerchief to Pierre. According to Pierre, the deceased man's death was very strange. He was sitting at his desk, and the handkerchief lay open on his lap. A red quill pen had been deeply thrust into his eyes. I translated the poem for Pierre. He was stunned for a few seconds, and his eyes seemed at first doubtful, then suddenly enlightened. When I asked him again about the case, he refused to say any more.

[11]
You are the last person
And you die in the room
You blink this eye
Suddenly
Some things are happening
Yes indeed, your hairs
Wake up and control the world

○ ○ ○   Why did the *Kute* band suddenly disappear whilst they were at
their strongest? Most probably nobody in the world knows why. All
that we know about them is that which has been recorded in writing.
This poem is the last one handed down by the *Kute* band itself. It is
said that when the executioner dealt with the victim's hairs, something unimaginable happened. Of course, it was just an account by
a detective. However, when the case was analyzed further, Peter
Crown, the inspector in charge of dealing with cases concerning the
Kute band, suddenly declared the case closed.

[12]
The explosion lasted until June
After striking the evils of scattering
People in the universe heard
The last voice
He walked a long, long way
Where did he go?

○ ○ ○   This is a Russian poem. It appeared in the *Podkamennaya Newspaper* the day before the Tunguska explosion which happened on
June 30, 1908. The author is unknown.

[13]

The masterpiece of the knights' mechanical rev-
olution
To destroy the city with black smoke
I have told you, you should be obsessed with
keeping silent
Then the Pope passes away

○ ○ ○   The events mentioned here happened in 64 AD, under the rule of

Nero, when Rome, the eternal city, experienced a great fire. The fire

started in the arena and lasted six days and seven nights. Only four

of the fourteen districts of Rome remained intact. Nero was furious

when he heard about it. He thought it was a plot by the Christians, so

he started to persecute them. What he did not realise was that some

residents discovered at the location where the fire started—the centre

of the arena—something strange: wheel gears, perfect and very pre-

cise wheel gears.

When I was staying in Rome, I thought of a way to find an ex-

traordinary collector who was able to find such wheel gears for me:

"You can see the incredibly sophisticated workmanship. Gears of this

size can only be discovered from the eighteenth century onwards...

judging from the mechanical structure, it is very hard to believe that

they could have been discovered in Ancient Rome. Look at the stur-

diness of the joints and the glass covering of the main body! It's in-

credible." He also showed me an ancient book, the diary of a resident

of Rome at that time. I discovered the above poem in the diary. It was written three years after the fire. It was probably a more crafted version, expressing his experiences before the fire. He had written, "Just before the disaster, I saw a member of the cavalry. He must have been very rich, for his body was covered with silver armour. There were only a few intriguing mechanical structures and transparent objects exposed… It was very late and I was the only one in the street. He told me to keep silent. His voice was husky and not very fluent, as if rusty metal objects were rubbing againgst each other…"

The entry for that day came to an abrupt end, and there are charred marks on the paper. The author of the diary escaped, but unfortunately died in the subsequent persecution of Christians. Pope Peter was also killed in the same persecution.

[14]
The way to the universe
Is, however, just a farmhouse
A relic from *Lannar*
And yet a great story

○ ○ ○   This poem is about a local legend from Liechtenstein. It is al-
leged that as early as 1723, Liechtenstein had a secret organization
of architects. Members of the organization at that time were astron-
omers and alchemists, and they were called *Lannar*. It is said that
this farmhouse was built half way up a hill, and when the door of the
farmhouse was pushed open, you could see the minutest grain on the
moon. It is said that the ruins of the house were discovered by local
inhabitants in the twentieth century, but the house was completely
empty except for some fragments of glass and traces of large equip-
ment. Therefore, scientists speculate that the effect described in the
poem might have been achieved by some optical means.

[15]
Silent in the morning
At nightfall
Give it an answer

○ ○ ○   This is a slogan for the "fill in encyclopedia on your own" campaign which was popular in France for a very short time in the nineteenth century. The entries in such a encyclopedia had only titles but not any specific contents. So readers needed to select an entry in the morning and fill in the specific contents of the entry after one day's research. But because of the excessive amount of work involved, this "fill in encyclopedia on your own" trend soon became obsolete, and only its skillfully contrived slogan survived.

[16]
Try to disappear
Understand the unpredictable
Rules do not exist

Words created by the desert
Floating on the ice
Admirable and mountainous

∘ ∘ ∘　This poem was published in the newspaper *Woke,* which was popular in Eastern Europe in the early eighteenth century. When European science had not yet reached a high level, some people wanted to be opportunistic by trying to invent a drug to make themselves invisible. They thought that they could thus evade military service and taxes. Lawless members of society also wanted to have the opportunity to disappear from the eye of the law forever. What was laughable was that some people thought they had successfully invented a drug to make them invisible, so they took the drug and set off on a round-the-world trip. They never imagined that every poem or note they wrote, and even their naked bodies, could be seen by everyone.

[17]
Sometimes a book falls asleep quietly
The wind gently breathes the air
It slowly opens petals and eyelids, like the Ve-
netian rose
But people do not see anything
The blue soul of Jupiter is as soft as velvet
Sometimes spending the best Part of a day in the
sunlight

Each cloud has its own harp
Colours sparkle on the edges of the high clouds
People are astonished at this awesome light
They close their eyes
They stare earnestly
The sunshine explodes over the sea
Artillery, fireworks and dynamite!

Then tonight the turbulent light becomes calm
The horizon is round, beautiful and blue
Within, it contains the dazzling panorama of the
world
But the island of the dead will never rise again
This is the meaning of life

∘ ∘ ∘   This is a Greek poem and its date is unknown. It describes a book belonging to a branch of the Gnostic sect, which records all the guilty souls in the world. Allegedly in a future day of judgment (called the day of death by believers), the book will be used to measure the good and evil of a person's life.

The first verse of the poem depicts the book in a fantastic touch, in which the phrase "the blue soul of Jupiter" reflects the animism of this sect. The second verse is a description of the day of death. The final verse is a sublimation, expressing an opinion on the meaning of life, but its specific connations are difficult to analyze textually.

P.S. The interesting fact is that in this church sect, the day of judgment is not "final" but recurrent. But what we can infer is that every time it occurs, it will cause calamity.

[18]
My head aches!
It is a terrible headache!
He says he has a headache
But it is never a calamity
If he is not stupid
Then he must be lying
Because my small, weak soul
Faces imminent death

○ ○ ○   I found this poem in 1967, in an early seventeenth century German castle, during my travels in Germany. The castle's owner, Augustus, was a legendary public figure at the time because he had been on good terms with some missing local celebrities before they disappeared. The poem was discovered in a secret chamber in the cellar of the castle. The discovery was made because a loose brick in one of its outer walls had been inadvertently removed by a former visitor. When the chamber was opened, archaeologists found that the formal entrance to the chamber was in a well near the castle. There was nothing in the chamber except this poem, so it was not possible to speculate about the function of the chamber.

[19]
In some world
Half the people absorb photovoltaic pressure
from its core
In light of our great society
He has not changed
People breathed a sigh of relief with a united
voice
In that world, he may have died already

∘∘∘ The poem was written in 1939, when Nazi Germany was at the height of its power. The author of this poem was a Nazi scientist at that time. His name was Dr. Baldu Edman. The author was perhaps using this poem to allude to the social phenomenon that the will of Nazi German leaders had replaced personal or individual thinking at that time. The use of the word "he" in the poem is suspected to be the author's own projection. According to the diary of Dr. Edman's assistant, Eckhard Zemmerman, Dr. Edman fled to the United States one year after the poem was written.

[20]
Cold weather in late autumn
Twisting the pallid sky
Thousands of students hurry by
Bending over to resist the breeze

A stone wall, looking at his face
He is a runner always pursuing acceleration
Pharaoh impaled him
He surrendered to Pharaoh's teaching
Then he broke the silence with a screech

○ ○ ○   In 1981, I was invited to attend the seventieth anniversary of the University of Iceland. I heard several alumni who had graduated in 1944 talk about this poem. Actually, it was written by them after a murder that caused a stir throughout the whole school.

Because the University of Iceland had just established its campus in 1940, it borrowed some exhibits from museums in Europe and displayed them in the basement of the new campus for students to learn something from them. These exhibits included an Egyptian sarcophagus from the British Museum, several Indian gemstone rings, a couple of paintings from the Louvre in France, and several sets of armour, including long spears, from the Armour Museum in Austria. They were not very rare exhibits or exhibits of great value, but it was unusual to see such exhibits in Iceland. The several alumni mentioned above just enrolled in 1940, so they were able to visit the exhibition which lasted only one week and was forced to close after the murder.

The scene on that day was as described in the first verse of the poem. The sky was white and gentle breezes were blowing. After the murder took place, all the students were immediately taken away from the teaching building. Although no one saw the scene of the murder with their own eyes, rumours quickly began to spread. It was said that the victim was a member of the school athletics team. He had no knowledge of history and had queried the existence of the four ancient civilizations many times in school. Ironically, he died next to the Egyptian sarcophagus, pierced by a spear from the Austrian armour. Later the police pronounced the incident to be a "murder where the perpetrator has not yet been caught", but many students in the same grade thought it to be the curse of Pharaoh, which we can read about in the poem by these alumni.

[21]

I don't know anything at all
Your pole is locked up in the box
There's a hacker and a dealer
I didn't agree to meet up

○ ○ ○   This verse was found in Berlin. It was in 1988, during the Cold War, when Germany was the front line for the intelligence struggle between the two blocs. In fact, it was not a poem, but a fragmented sound recording which someone had transcribed. Local people told me that this was a conversation recorded by a spy eavesdropping on an interrogation at the police station. The first and third sentences were uttered by the arrested person, and the second and fourth sentences were spoken by the police. "Pole" was a slang word from the then East German underground market, referring to rifles.

[22]
Please wait a minute
Before the lake collapses
The silence of the second frost
Establishing the purpose of the roses
Never ever let them know
That you hate the sun
Yes, it's true, at that time
I was the sun

∘ ∘ ∘   This is a Russian poem, found on a stone wall in the Ural Mountains. The poem is skillfully written, recounting part of a local myth
in the voice of the sun god: whenever winter came, on the highest
mountains in the world, a cluster of roses would grow. The growth
and death cycles of the roses coincided with the whole length of
winter (from beginning to end). During the last days of winter, their
petals would fall with the wind, and would be carried through the
boundless land, trying to find a book that recorded the souls of sin-
ners. The arrival of each petal indicated that another 9,800 souls
would be judged. The petals would not stop falling until the spring.
The second line of the poem —"Before the lake collapses"— refers
to the thawing of the snow. Local villagers told me that there had
been a year in which winter lasted so long that petals fell as if they
were infinite. A few years later, Mongolians arrived from the East

and the army killed many of the local inhabitants. People said that all those people died because too many petals had flown into the book of records.

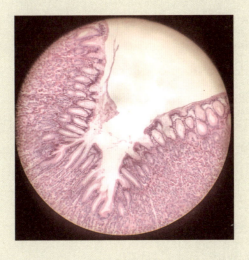

[23]

I remember this morning

A bright morning

I ran behind some children

Under our feet there was soft soil and grass, dancing in the wind

The sun seemed to us to be of a soft color

We were like lambs by the river

We came to a dilapidated temple

I saw some great deities

They seemed to have been there for a long time

However, they were in the process of dying

That night, a storm had just passed by

Dark clouds were like rolling smoke in the sky

I sat in the pond behind the house, amid the damp landscape

A strange man came over to me

He was dressed in black

As a black flag fluttered against a dark sky

He said I should persevere for this day

A special day in this infinite universe

It was only then that I realized

This winter is eternal

They are like boats

Like my veins, my neck
I have a lot of twisted ropes, and I will never be
able to untwist them
Red Robin died on the golden acacia tree
Finally, I die for my own sake

○ ○ ○   In 1990, an Orthodox church in Astrakhan, Russia, was demolished and rebuilt. Workers found the poem engraved on a silver board in its foundation and asked me to determine its origin. I translated the poem and found a specific detail: the construction materials of the foundation were obviously older and coarser than those used in the church itself. At my request, they cleaned the soil carefully, then I found a Gnostic gathering place buried underground. The church that was built later was actually used to conceal signs of heresy. My friend, Sir Willis of Imperial College, London, suggested that this poem perhaps describes events that happened after the day of judgment, according to their religion, the day of their death. "Storm" implies the day of death, "dark clouds" and "smoke" could mean the tragedy after their trial. The strange man in black found the narrator and invited him to "continue the special day in the infinite universe". This sentence comes from local folklore that said that a one-eyed man in black would go hunting for young boys, asking them if they wanted to "continue the special day in the infinite universe". If the boy agreed, the one-eyed man would use magic art that spread an orange-red flame to take his soul, and imbue his consciousness into the boy's body to achieve immortality, but unfortunately, the state of having only one eye would remain forever: after the transposing of each soul, an accident would happen that caused one of his eyes to disappear.

The last part of the poem is easier to understand, telling the story of a terrified person (perhaps the poet himself) who committed suicide in despair because he foresaw the day of death. "I have a lot of twisted ropes, and I will never be able to untwist them" clearly reflects the protagonist who is experiencing a painful struggle; the vein and neck image also implies a final end. But there are stiu some puzzling words in this poem that have a pressing need of an explanation.

The acacia tree is native to tropical America and is still only found in the tropics. Even though Astrakhan is in the very south of Russia, it is still impossible to grow acacia trees there. But when I did some research, I found the notes of a scholar from Georgia. He claimed that the region experienced an abnormal temperature rise in the twelfth century which lasted for thirty years. Although the growth cycle of the acacia tree is very long, it is possible for it to grow in this amount of time. So the "golden acacia" in the poem may not be a living tree, but a hand carving handed down from that era.

The eternal winter is a mythical story, which would naturally have spread from the Ural region to Astrakhan. The myth describes how one of the gods punishes a hero who tries to challenge his authority by grabbing hold of the sunshine. The long winter resulted in the death of innumerable innocent creatures. The purpose of this allusion here is unclear, perhaps just to show off the author's knowledge, or to suggest that the day of death is more terrible than the eternal winter.

P.S. There are many local rumors about magic arts. In addition, there are folk myths about "swallowing pearls to live forever" or "painting mirrors pink to cure diseases". My good friend Stanley Marsh's book *The Lost Story* gives more details of these.

[24]
Behind the bridge
There is naked frost
The dark monsoon
I will die in the sun

○ ○ ○   In 1832, in order to remove the rock barriers that impeded ship-
ping in the Rhine River, relevant public officials decided to blow up
two waterways in Bingen, Germany. In the course of opening up the
second channel, a bridge was destroyed. At each of the four corners
of the bridge there was a stone gargoyle statue, which is rare in bridge
design. The bridge surfaces were destroyed without the approval of
the cultural authorities. The four stone gargoyle statues were also
broken up. This event did not come to light until 1982. According to
documents concerning the event, workers had discovered a piece of
parchment in the head of the stone gargoyle at the southeast corner of
the bridge. The above poem was written on the parchment.

[25]
A Philosophy
A language
A fish
A world
But it rained
All things on earth are not eternal
Then
I will exist no longer

o o o　This poem was found in the ruins of a palace in Cordoba, Spain. Spain (known as Andalusia by the Arabs) was ruled by an Islamic regime for a long period, reaching the pinnacle of the world politically, militarily and culturally. It is assumed that the poem was written in a hybrid language that contained both Spanish and Arabic, during the Sultanate of Umayyad. The exact location where the poem was discovered was next to a collapsed building, and it was recorded on papyrus. From the handwriting and signature, it can be inferred that it was a scholar's informal philosophical essay, discussing the dialectical relationship between the eternity of all things and his own existence. The palace was later burned down. Fortunately, the poem was wedged beneath the building and survived.

[26]
The black moon hanging over the mountains
Radiates an astonishing red light
The wind is speaking in the woods
I know not what that language is

The blue crow brought his letter
On dark green tea paper of wax and foam
Twisted strokes and strange lines
I know not what that language is

He cannot possibly be there
In ancient temples in the desert
Wind is blown by the sand
I know not what that language is

∘ ∘ ∘   This poem, in Icelandic, was found on a rock along the northwest coast. It was written in the eighteenth century, describing the
enormous power of a spell. The scenery and imagery are believed to
be the effect caused by this "I know not what" language. Natives of
the area say that if a devout monk recites these words, he can "erad-
icate the most fragile existence with the most powerful energy", like
feathers, clothes, books and so on.

P.S. The original text may have been tampered with, because the
second sentence on the stone has erasure marks, by which it can be
deduced that "red light" should be "orange light".

[27]
You have already found what you wanted
Let us enact a law for my death
Cannon, bait, kidneys
My heart is my mother's embrace

○ ○ ○   This poem comes from an old twelfth-century sheepskin scroll. It talks about the battle between Viking pirates and Indians. The former have just set foot on the American continent and think they have finally acquired a bountiful base camp. Although the results of carbon-14 measurements are consistent with archaeologists' estimates, the word "cannon" (Kanoner) in the poem, similar to the modern Nordic language family, has attracted the attention of academic circles.

[28]
From one year to another
I have already suffered
You will too
He is behind you

∘ ∘ ∘   Legend has it that these are the dying words that King Edward I
of England spoke to his son.

[29]
I am you
The black sky and I
Drink as much as you will
Depart from God
Seize your country
You are gone
Everything is over
Including time itself

○ ○ ○   In the sixth century BC, Ireland had six kingdoms in its territory, one of which had a ruler called Malloy. Malloy liked drinking very much and often did some unimaginable things when he was drunk. This poem was written after his last bout of drunkenness, when he ordered his troops to attack his own kingdom. Because his men knew that it was a capital offence to go against the king's will, they carried out his orders.

[30]
Respected Mr. Salt Water
—— Wish him a long life!
This is his mantra:

"There I am
It's nice to meet you
Knight in the fog"

Magicians distill planets
The mineral goddess hates the moon
They went to the shore with Mr. Salt Water
To destroy the dark Utopia

○ ○ ○   In 79 AD, Mount Vesuvius erupted, and the great ancient city of Pompeii was instantly submerged by volcanic ash. Discovered on a mud slab in a magnificent hall, this poem probably describes the adventures of several people.

There is nothing special about the content of this poem, but it is interesting that although the hall was located very close to the volcano, it was the last to be buried. Some wheel gears were found near to the mud slab. A map of Pompeii was painted on the front wall of the hall, which was destroyed by people, and the scratches were filled with salt and rust. On the top of the map, words were written in human blood in an ancient religious language. The words said, "This is the dark Utopia."

[31]
The belated torment opened the old tree in the
attic
The leaves are asleep in my lower bunk bed
Turn off the lights and the room suddenly shines
Darkness lies in infinite green eyes
I caught sight of screams

Green leaves grow from coffee forgotten outside
Covered by a layer of snow with purple spots
The heavy yoke of the sun is like a book
It will crack, drink it carefully and you will see it
I took the folds out of the book and put them
back in my mouth

I am searching for it
But it cannott be found
It is just water
Blue, gold and red rust
The pink, floating head of a man

The light above my head is dazzling me
Pick up the lock
Sigh and smile:
"Where is
The final valve?"

○ ○ ○　　This poem was found among the effects of the Portuguese writer Marcos Mello after his death in 1964. The poem was written in 1923, when Marcos Mello was about to start his second novel, *Cairo Night*. Consequently he went to visit the grandson of Umulan Adurashid, a famous nineteenth-century Egyptian novelist, for inspiration. This poem was written for him on his journey. Some of the images such as "green eyes" and "coffee" have appeared in the works of Umulan Adurashid.

[32]
Now you have died
On her body
You are this person's ringleader
An invisible person
Sorrowful poems
Never die

∘∘∘   The last leader of the *Die Wolke* cult was a young woman. It was said that when she was young she leaked the secret of the energy trans formation ceremony. This indirectly led to the disintegration of the cult. At the time of the disbanding of this organization, many critics from outside "civilized society" were pleased with this outcome. But ignorant members of the cult thought that this person had destroyed the altar for energy transformation, and firmly believed that the people who had passed away there had really become eternal matter in the universe. This is a poem left by a member of the cult as a lament.

[33]
On the ice in the desert
I triumphed
In a feverish carnival
I lost my life

○ ○ ○   Snow fell once again in Algiers in 1979. For the first time, the
temperature in the hottest part of the world fell below freezing point.
The unprepared Algerian people were exposed to extreme cold. This
titleless poem was discovered in 1981, written on a piece of letter
paper, which was perfectly packed in a small blue box. It can be seen
from the handwriting that the author was extremely excited at the
time. There are traces of deletion in the last sentence. The revised
handwriting is very sloppy, and some letters have even been crossed
out with one stroke. I like the poem and its background very much,
but I cannot fathom out the author's psychological state as he wrote
the last sentence (even though an old friend of mine who studied psy-
chology deduced that this person may have died of a heart attack).

[34]

This is the situation

There are all kinds of particles

They can only be obtained at high temperatures

Like the sun in the sky

On the exterior organometallic veins, they initiated the human world

On the shore of life, people see four-dimensional particles

If you go beyond the limits, you can digest physical power

∘ ∘ ∘   In the summer of 1984, at the Reykjavik Municipal Library, I found a book entitled *Polarization of Light* by British physicist William Spottiswoode. Personally, I do not know much about physics, but I was attracted by the large number of exquisite hand-drawn illustrations in this book. They seemed to be drawings of patterns of light observed by the author through special instruments. Some of these patterns were circular and some were symmetrical along an oblique axis, which I found to be interesting. Because the book was not very thick (only 130 pages), I quickly read it in a superficial manner. When I came to the last page, I found a page that had been deliberately left blank, but someone had scribbled a few lines on it. At first I thought it was a commentary left by a former borrower, but after careful examination, I realized that it was actually a poem which included many scientific terms.

The poem has no signature, so it is impossible to investigate who the author is. But there is a date at the end of the poem: August 3, 1876. This date makes the poem very interesting. What one needs to know here is that in the nineteenth century, the four-dimensional theory was totally unacceptable to most people. So the fact that a man in Iceland wrote a poem in Icelandic in 1876, containing the word "four-dimensional", is truly amazing.

This poem seems to revolve around some kind of particle which has very strong energy. I cannot help thinking about atomic energy. But as far as I know, the theory of atomic energy was put forward long after the poem was written, and it has nothing to do with the "four dimensions" described in the poem. Therefore, my theory has no ground to stand on. Since I am not a scientist and the logic of this poem is not so solid, I have not as yet come up with a better explanation. It is also unclear as to why the poem appears on the back page of *Polarization of Light*.

[35]
Oh, my dearest
Looting everything
Then going to Basque
And playing the organ
With Aldo's vicious hissing
Produces
Peace and sunshine

○ ○ ○　This poem, written in the Basque language, was found on a
church altar in Bilbao, the largest city in the Basque Autonomous
Region. It was written by a medieval nobleman who loved the organ,
after he led the cavalry to loot the territory of the "betrayer" Aldo. He
wrote it down to express his joy.

[36]
You say you are here
To get more possessions
Do not leave me out
Let's enjoy the blue flame in the dark
Fate and death are worthless

○ ○ ○   This poem was found in a mountainous village in Bavaria. The
poem comes from a passage of prose written by a nihilistic philosopher. It was then transformed by local villagers into a poem. They
also added an element of mysticism.

[37]
You say you are here
The destruction of churches
Causes the world to be no more
Clean nights
Wine and
 Magnificent philosophy

○ ○ ○   Written in the fifteenth century, this poem tells of a fire at a church in Norway. The annals of local history show that the church was built by a group of mystics from Denmark, who claimed to have received a dying king's estate. Local residents witnessed the construction process, describing it as "puzzling" as some of its structures seemed normal at first glance, but upon careful observation, revealed dizzying shapes. The church existed for about 120 years, until one day a "one-eyed man in black clothes" arrived there, and there seemed to be some dispute with the people in the church. According to local history, the man shouted to the priest of the church, "I'll take back what belongs to me." "Yes, I'm of the sixth generation!" Finally he "swore and went away, leaving behind an obnoxious atmosphere". That night, the church was set on fire with orange flames. Local residents were shocked and tried to salvage the building (the church was near the centre of the town), but were only able to recover a few bottles of wine and some books.

No one in the church survived.

I asked to see the pages that remained of the books. They were written in a mixture of Danish, Hebrew, ancient Phoenician ,and some hard-to-identify religious symbols. There were many rose petals in the books.

Vanishing Poems

○
○

Poems from the Asia-Pacific Region

The Asia-Pacific region includes Asia and the areas on the coast of the Pacific Ocean. My short visits have not allowed me to collect too many satisfactory works, so the quantity of Asia-Pacific poems included here is not very large. But they triumph with their magnificent imagery and fantastic imagination, which at the same time contain profound philosophical implications.

○
○

[1]
You are an angry God
You and your fellow gods made use of the set-
ting sun but achieved nothing
Then the cure continues
God is infinite

∘ ∘ ∘   This poem, which was discovered in Israel, is believed to be a
translation. The original text is no longer available, but according to
the *Heresy Trial Book*, a book recording literary works "destroyed
because of their excessive evil", the original text Should have been a
maxim of a branch of the Gnostic sect.

This maxim seems to be deviant. Firstly, it uses "you" to speak
to God. Secondly, when it refers to God, it also refers to his "fellow
gods". Thirdly, it accuses God of "achieving nothing". Or it can be
put in this way, as a maxim belonging to a heretic Christian sect (in
any case it is part of Christianity), only the last part of the poem
can be interpreted as praise to God. My friend, Sir Willis from Imperial College, London, came up with an interesting theory. In the
first two lines, the word "God" does not signify the true God, but is
a self-conceited, other divine being, possibly the "Master Creator"
who created the material world according to the Gnostic doctrine.
Although at the time my friend was speaking sarcastically about his
theory ("Just mention it casually," he said, "you'd better not write it
down."), I nevertheless think that it is an ingenious explanation. It
is quite possible that some distortion has taken place in the process

of translation. In the first half of the poem, the word "God" refers to the creator of the material world. The "God" in the second half of the poem refers to the creator of a more noble and sacred spiritual world. The Gnostic sect always believed that only by extinguishing the body could liberation be achieved, which accounts for the mild contempt for the Master Creator of the material world.

The original poem was written in the third century or so, and was burned during a purge of heresy in the thirteenth century. However, it was later translated and recorded. Some of the survived followers of this sect fled northwards to the "Straits Land" (presumably Constantinople), some went to a "Turkic land" (probably near Turkey) and others fled to "Mongolian-covered areas" (the Volga River Basin). I made some fruitless attempts to find the offspring of these people by going through endless genealogies and yellow pages.

The "setting sun" mentioned in the poem may refer to an object, as recorded in the *Heresy Trial Book*. It is described as "shining with evil light, having the colour when the sun is setting and the Lord's light is leaving the earth". Some Gnostic documents say that this object was acquired by an immortal prophet from the sun: "The immortal boneless man climbed the highest mountain, to the sun [illegible] then [illegible], God's great hand appears and [illegible]. So the infinite setting sun fell into the hands of the boneless man, who was also robbed of the ability to walk and one of his eyes, as punishment for stealing the pure fire of God...Because of the pure fire, he can avoid death's [impossible to make out] and live forever, as long as the fire is still in his hands."

[2]
You have already drowned
Do not worry
Come to the ancestral temple
And drink water

∘∘∘   The poem comes from a Maori tribe called Manaia. Manaia, in
local legends, was a god with a bird's head and a human body. The
tribe is composed of three clans: the Ma, the Na and the Ia. The three
ancestral temples in the tribal centre reflect the perfect clan system
of the tribe. The Manaians believed that everything in the ancestral
temples contained the powerful energy of the ancestor's soul, so after
people drowned, the Manaians would bring the drowned person to
his or her ancestral temple and give him or her "holy water" to purify
the "filthy water" in the body of the drowned person.

[3]

Dark gold is the colour of the old rock and roll music

The sun lies in the sunshine

I do not know whether this film comes from the piano

Music comes from clear solar streams and reduces its flames in the afternoon

Everything in the green mirror is futile

But the summer, the scorching summer, dreams of rest

∘ ∘ ∘ That year I was in Aden, Yemen's largest city. It was summer, and the temperature seemed to melt everything. I escaped to a market to avoid the sun and got some shade under the roof of a shop, only to find that the place was selling antiques. I walked along endless pavements, enjoying looking at a wide range of goods, including luxurious Persian carpets, Swahilian ivory and pearls, Indian gems and Chinese porcelain. I even saw some Roman stone carvings. Among all the merchandise, the one thing that fascinated me most was a piece of brocade, on which a poem in Arabic was embroidered, using fine gold thread. When I asked the shopkeeper where the poem came from, he said proudly, "Sir, I composed it myself. The first, third and fifth lines are my own work; and the second, fourth and sixth lines came from a folk legend. This legend tells a story about summer. It tells us that in the remote southern desert, there are many suns, which are bathed in each other's sunshine. These giant planets are so hot that the rays emitted by them are extremely clear, just like pure flames.

[4]
Will you wait for me?
I don't care
Wait a while longer, I will too
Where are you?

○ ○ ○   This is a Japanese verse, found in the trunk of a car. It was carved
on the metal frame of the car using fingernails. The car was manu-
factured in South Africa and arrived in Japan from Durban Port in a
container.

[5]
The haste of winter
Is almost impossible to predict
She is from Livia
Welcome to the world of love!

An unpredictable language
A stubborn and immortal gap
King of Heaven
Do you not think that you are the ruler?

You are the one who is cursing yourself
You can hide evil
The sin of death is truth
You cannot just hide it

Whatever your life is
You do not want to break your embrace
Why not?
You know how to ruin your life

○ ○ ○   This poem was found in the Horqin grassland and the verses
were inscribed on a stone tablet. The outer layer of the stone tablet was translucent and was probably made of some special crystal.
There were also some rose petals embedded in it. The poem was
probably written around the twelfth century. It begins with a descrip-

tion of the sudden and unpredictable arrival of winter, followed by two sentences that are too difficult to understand. Taking into consideration the contents of the second and third verses, it can be inferred that the poet intends to use this poem to express his reflections on death. He believes that neither the prophecy nor the "immortal gap" nor the King of Heaven can escape it.

[6]

We walked on both sides of the sunny square

Our twisted shadows could be seen on the hous-
es along the way

It was like going past a key

Slowly flowing is the road built of square stones

All thoroughly roasted people rise up from the
sun

Soft as velvet

Fortunately bursting into nothingness

∘ ∘ ∘　The poem was discovered in an ancient Iraqi city. A small vendor

insisted on selling me a fine Ottoman painting. I bought it reluctantly,

only to find the poem embroidered on its interlayer. I asked local

people about it, and they said the poem described the destruction of

a city in the remote southern desert. It is said that the sun there is so

hot, so intensely hot, that on one summer day, a heat wave melted the

ground surface. The people there were all roasted alive, and reached

the sun with the rising hot air. Because the heat was so intense that it

melted everything except human souls, their sins were washed away

by the heat, and they "entered into nothingness happily".

[7]

He lit up the sea and wine
He will burn the gods and cut them off
He brought the sun into the fog
He did not know what the sky was
Because heaven definitely did not exist

However, winter is always infinite

○ ○ ○   The poem was found on a stone tablet on the Xilingol grassland.
The mythical "he" was a fighter who challenged the gods. In the
course of the battle, the grassland was ignited (the sea in the poem
was interpreted as grassland, because the endless and grandiose ter-
rain is like the sea). According to the local legend, "In their epic
battle, the earth became bright; after the [the next word is unrecog-
nizable] victory, it began to rain with the smell of wine." At the same
time, the sun was blocked by fog for several months (giving rise to
dramatic changes in grassland conditions, resulting in the deaths of
large numbers of livestock through starvation). In the end, the unknown hero won. He killed the gods, but at the same time brought disaster to the people. "However, winter is always infinite" is believed
to be censure of his irresponsible behavior. His great-grandson was
thus distrusted, deprived of the glory of battle during the Mongolian
Western Expedition, and assigned the duty of guarding the Volga
River Basin; therefore, he had a gloomly end.

My friend, Sir Willis of Imperial College in England, found some interesting accounts in the records of a traveller in the late Liao Dynasty in China. The traveler was exploring the northern frontier of the empire, now known as the Xing'an Mountains. He watched a mountain "burst in the upper part, orange-red; smoke billowed, shading the sky", and then he felt breathless, and after rinsing his nose with river water, he felt somewhat better. Sir Willis believes that this is a description of the eruption of a volcano, and that it should be the A'ershan volcano. The volcano is very close to where the poem was found, so the scenes depicted in the poem, such as the grassland being ignited and the sun being out of sight, could all be the result of a volcanic eruption. Personally, I agree with this explanation.

[8]

At that time, our city

Was riding in darkness, sinking deeper and deeper

It had the colours of gray iron and fog

The great God burned up the moon

And the day immediately fell into a whirlpool

After a while, it became dark and invisible

Then he fell into the night

He fell into his good night sleep

○ ○ ○ Angkor, the great capital of the Khmer Kingdom, began to decline in the fifteenth century, deteriorating from a regional metropo-
lis to an abandoned relic in the jungle. The poem, written in ancient
Khmer, was found on a statue of Buddha in Angkor Wat, roughly
carved with certain metallic tools. This Buddha statue is in a relatively remote location. I could well believe that no one else except
for myself has been there in recent decades. These beautiful statues
are beginning to rust. On the stone wall next to the Buddha statue
are inscriptions by local inhabitants complaining that the whole sky
was disappearing, that the sun and moon were invisible, and that
darkness was enveloping the city: they had to leave the place. This
is consistent with historical records. Angkor did not decline in an
instant, but over a long period of time.

[9]
It's too hot
I love water
So much water
How extremely hot it is
Asphalt as water
I long for water
Let's get your water
Pour out your water
I'm going to drink water

○ ○ ○   This is a poem written by Ichiro Matsuda, a Japanese water enthusiast. Ichiro Matsuda suffers from a rare disease that causes extreme dryness, heat and thirst. He turns the disease into a hobby,
travelling around the world to taste various drinks. This poem fully
reflects his obsession with water. It is said that he copies it three
times a day.

[10]
First job
The fountain is dreary
That's because of its
Foggy eyebrows
The disappearance of initial shyness
Break a bullet
Let's face reality
Let's say goodbye

○ ○ ○   This is the suicide note of Japanese horticultural designer, Koto Kohei. After ten years of careful preparation, he participated in the first fountain design competition and designed a fountain system that could display human faces. It was supposed to be a great design, but because the fountain was too large, the droplets could not successfully form the eyebrows of the face. This resulted in an unenthusiastic response to the system. Ultimately it did not win any awards. Koto Kohei was very disappointed and ended his life with a pistol. The fountain design competition was never held again.

Vanishing Poems

○
○
○

African Poems

There are countless lost poems in ancient Africa. From the fertile delta of Egypt to the deserts of Sudan, from the coast of Benin to the dense forests of Congo, from the plateau of Kenya to the desert of South Africa, one ancient line after another echoes through the endless land.

○
○
○

[1]
Beautiful season
It disappeared out of sight
We can fly
I wish you good luck

∘ ∘ ∘   This poem comes from the Tayalan tribe in the Drakensburg Mountains of southern Africa. The word *"Tayalan"* means "flying" in the tribal language, which is closely related to the tribal migration habits. At the end of Drakensburg's beautiful autumn season (around March each year), the mountains are finally unable to withstand the effects of humid and cold air masses from the southeast, and temperatures drop dramatically. Since the *Tayalan* tribe was unable to survive the cold at the end of each year, they would begin, from around December, to collect huge leaves and a large number of branches from ancient trees to build the aircraft needed for migration journey. According to textual research, these self-designed aircraft did not have a fixed style. In fact, these aircraft were made using the unique weaving skills of their tribe. The tribe would transport large quantities of leaves, branches and a natural adhesive to the top of the mountain near *Mohotlon* and assemble them firmly so that they could support them and enable them to ues updraft to fly about 300 kilometers after take-off. The *Tayalan* tribe worked in groups. They usually flew north together in a few days after all the aircraft were made. At the end of each March, hundreds of aircraft glided together over the Drakensburg mountains.

The originality of aircraft is very important in the *Tayalan* culture, because they believe that the inspiration for constructing aircraft was given by their gods. If an aircraft used by the *Tayalan* failed to take off during the migration period, that person would be regarded as "unclean" and would face the punishment of being abandoned in the cold mountains. Therefore, the last sentence in the poem—"I wish you good luck"—is an expression of mockery towards the "unclean" by those who were able to fly with their fellow tribal members.

[2]
Pearls are lame
This is not easy
She is blue
Her colour has come too late
The pearl is crying

○ ○ ○   This poem is in Swahili. It was discovered in a tribe in the dense forests of Uganda. The most important word in the poem is the word "pearl". It is impossible to deduce what it really means. The description in the poem is also puzzling, for example the line, "Her color has come too late" and so on. I spoke to local people through an interpreter, and they said it was just a poem written for fun.

[3]
The coffee is cooling
This gentleman is crying
You dream of mourning
Let's put you here
Purple leaves
A martyred blade
In the middle of the house
You killed the scientist

○ ○ ○   This poem was found amongst the manuscripts of the nineteenth-century Egyptian writer, Umulan Adurashid. The author is
famous for his illusory style and his love of coffee. According to
legend, Adurashid cultivated a coffee bean which produced a hallucinogenic effect, and he drank the coffee made from this coffee bean
for inspiration. If this legend is true, the poem may well have been
written when the poet was in a hallucinatory state. The line, "You
killed the scientist", is suspected to be the inspiration for Adurashid's
later literary work, *Tut at Dusk*.

[4]
You let slip
All of your time
You cried
I became crazy
I have no time
It is time to change
And then
I died

○ ○ ○   This poem was found in Abuja, Nigeria. It is written in the Mandinka language. It is highly literary and is engraved on several musical instruments. It is worth noting that the language is not used locally.

[5]

There is no time
I have no purpose
I will become a fierce gale
I cut a room open
I killed the bird
And disappeared

○ ○ ○ This poem was found in a crack in the wall of the ancient city of Timbuktu, Mali, and is written in the Mandinka language. I asked an eminent imam in the temple, and he told me that this style of writing probably would be the work of a bard during the Mali Empire. It is presumed that the poem was written out of overflowing inspiration during worship time, and was hastily forgotten in the cracks of the wall. The word "room" may refer to the poet's inner world, and the "bird" may refer to his sins.

[6]
This is the only thing you can do:
Do not steal pearls

Pearls are easy to make
But when it goes crazy, it falls asleep, in juice
When the pearls are reddish
I do not know how to get rid of him

When pearls broke down their flames
I killed your pain
When the black pearl leaves burn
This is the only way to achieve immortality
Do not steal pearls
This is the only thing you can do

○ ○ ○   This poem is in Swahili. It was found on Zanzibar Island and
passed down orally among urban residents. It is said that during the
former Sultanate of Kilwa, Zanzibar was the largest port in Africa,
with numerous ships and merchants coming and going. It also meant
that many strange beliefs and rituals came to the island. This poem
tells the story of a careless apprentice who accidentally made a big
mistake while studying mysticism with his master. The first part of
the poem is spoken in the earnest voice of the master, instructing his
apprentice. But the final ending is a profound reflection on the final
outcome of the apprentice.

The "pearl" is interpreted by local people as a creature made by a secret method. It is a white spherical object with appendages that seem to belong to a spider, but it curls up in the shape of a pearl. The sect that the apprentice belonged to tried to achieve a psychic effect through this "pearl".

When I was in Zanzibar, I bought a "pearl" from a local businessman and sent it to the Academy of Sciences for research. The final result informed me that it was just a common insect. The only special thing about it was that its blood contained nerve blockers, which can cause hallucinations which induce people to feel that time has slowed down. Whilst I was on the island I also found a broken skull, which had a scar from the left eyebrow to the right jaw. It must have had something to do with religious rituals.

[7]
The pumpkin is bleeding
Do not miss it
At dawn
Beautiful, beautiful

∘ ∘ ∘   Legend has it that the souls of the dead will visit the world on the
Eve of Halloween, so people light lanterns to frighten away ghosts,
and at the same time illuminate the path for ghosts and guide them
back. Pumpkins are found to be perfect receptacles for lights, so the
use of pumpkins has spread. In 1975, in central Africa, a boy named
Jack fell asleep with his pumpkin in his hands on Halloween night.
The next morning, his mother found this poem only.

[8]
I do not know
No one knows how to die
I am sorry, I do not know

Somewhere in the sky——
That is where the sun goes down
He went to a small town
Screaming in the desert

No one knows how to die
But that is not really so
In any case, we are sorry
He knows how to die
He is with them, is with them

○ ○ ○   This poem is written in a dialect of the Amharic language. A towering tree was found in a desert valley in southeastern Ethiopia, and the poem was written on it in blood. After some investigation, I discovered that the "he" mentioned in the poem was a god in the local religion. It is said that "he" is also death's opponent, the "screamer". He can reverse the energy that is given to any person by the god of death. That is to say, in the eyes of the god of death, the dying man can continue to live for a long time by his hand, and those who are supposed to live a long and healthy life will die soon after they see him.

[9]
This cell is tragic
It is not part of hell

○ ○ ○   This poem was written in the Amharic language. At the time, I was visiting a local official in Ethiopia. One day he told me that their prophet had recently revived and asked me if I was interested in seeing him. I agreed, and he led me to a small stone house which was damp and dark, with foul air. In the innermost part of the house sat a shabby old man with a huge scar right across his face. "This man is an immortal", the officer said. "He has experienced endless historical events, and his wisdom is unparalleled." The two of us sat in front of the prophet, and the official kept asking him questions, recording carefully then reading out the words formed by the vague voice coming from the prophet's mouth. I saw the old man's eyes staring at me all the time.

As we left, the prophet stuffed a piece of papyrus into my hand, with surprising speed. It had this short poem written on it.

[10]
You cannot walk about!
It will never eat
Their ball has stopped
Go back

∘ ∘ ∘   I have traveled all over Africa except for the Sahara. Summer is the time when tens of thousands of animals thrive in the borders of the rare dense forests and savannah of Western Africa. For generations, the *Simba* people have used the tall fir trees here as the necessary resource for their lives, from building their homes to producing the handles of all kinds of appliances needed for daily living, and so on. The day after I arrived, I followed the tribesmen on foot to the cedar forests to record how they obtained their resources without relying on modern means. To my astonishment, these primitive tribesmen observed nature more meticulously than artists. Because the China fir trees here are not as dense as in the snow-covered forests in Russia, insects living on every small piece of land, once they become adults, will gather around a few nearby China fir trees to forage. The only guide who knew a little English told me that in their spare time, locals often paste clay and grass on their bodies and lie down beside the trees for a short time, to watch the wonderful hunting activities carried out by these very common insects for the sake of survival.

An elder accompanying me told me in their language what he had seen and heard in the woods when he was young. One summer night, he was resting there as he had done in the past. Contrary to what was usual, he suddenly saw a small amber stone carrying a mantis and a dead leaf butterfly, standing on a small slope. Two or three metres down the slope, an old mantis and a young mantis were casting covetous eyes, as if they wanted to fight for the dead leaf butterfly. After a long while, the two mantises did not wait long enough for the right moment. In fact, they wanted to mount their attacks when another young momtis was not paying attention, and then drag away the dead leaf butterfly and eat a good meal. However, they did not know about the existence of the amber globule around the dead butterfly. A hot wind blew, and the amber globule was shaken from the soil and began to move down the slope. The two mamtises waited for a moment, then quickly rushed up and tried to stab the dead leaf butterfly with their huge nippers, but did not touch it at all. After a half-minute standoff with the brown transparent ball, they finally gave up what seemed like a good meal. After witnessing this interesting scene, the elder immediately returned to the tribe and recorded it on papyrus. I heard this story, and I am telling it to you here. I hope you can also experience the touching scenes in this insignificant corner of nature.

[11]

The sun is in the sky, the sky is red
The heaven above is desolate
Blue pearls are black pearls in the sky
Pearls are purple and blue
This is a vagrant
A lonely island
Always alive

○ ○ ○   This poem was written in Swahili. It was discovered in a village

off the coast of Kenya. A local woodcarving shows the poet's image

in an extremely artistic way: tall and thin, with a black flame in his

hands and scars on his body. But the most striking part is the huge

scar across his face. He carried a lot of white spherical objects to

treat people's diseases. He stayed in the village for a long time until

he fell off a cliff one day.

[12]
I'm crazy
This is my wish
That's great for me
I grabbed my hair
I have a lot of money in my eyes
Pretty penny
I have always been here
I'm not here either
From here on
Please do not contact us at any time:
You can't do it

∘ ∘ ∘   This is a short poem found in a bunker in Algeria after World War II. The author, Kachasi Mate, was a prominent Jewish rich man in North Africa who made his fortune through mining in the 1940s. In order to escape the Nazi massacre, he built the bunker early in 1938 and sealed himself inside the bunker in 1941, staying there from morning till night. During this period of hiding himself, he changed his name to Barr Kibi and concealed his Jewish identity.

In 1982, archaeologists researched Kachasi's genealogy and discovered that his great-grandfather was born in Aachen, central Germany. The neat handwriting on his account records, showing the output, prices and tax records of various minerals, proved that he was a highly educated man.

He sold jadeites, black agates, emeralds and other minerals and was well-known throughout Europe. Even marble which he produced had been purchased by specialist traders in Europe. On July 10, 1942, *Kachasi* completed his last recorded black agate trade deal, and after that there was no more news of him. By the time the German army opened the door of the bunker on August 30, he had disappeared.

[13]
Bed lies down
It's easy to stay here this night
It's free
It's so easy to sleep
This is forever part of my life
This is the highest level of humour
It brings an end to almost every day

∘ ∘ ∘　This was the slogan of the folding bed brand *Fangmian*, which sold very well in Africa in 1982. The company adopted a twelve-hour working system.

[14]
This is the one you are seeking:
Let's cry and dance
It's easier for you
Let it rain
Let it become law
Let it become selfish
Let it become a pearl
Let it become our light

Loneliness!
Is the final death

This is a milestone
The sun burns in the eyes
The ocean is the head
Flames are the tail
Don't lose your brown colour

There is an oasis in the desert
There is a whale in the desert
There are three poets in the wilderness
There's a poet's tower
These pyramids lie amongst lies
Sadly
The oasis is about to die

The tower is about to fall
Thirty days, a kingdom
Easily devouring the moon:
——— Happiness

It doesn't matter
That's why it ended:
It's just above it
Read it

○ ○ ○   This long poem was found on a wall among the ruins in the city of Timbuktu, Mali, and was written in an ancient Songhai language. Timbuktu was probably one of the richest cities in the world in the fourteenth and fifteenth centuries. It was an important cultural, economic, commercial and religious centre in West Africa during the Malian and Songhai Empires. But from the time of the invasion of the Moroccans in the sixteenth century, this great city began to decline.

    The poem is carved on a mud wall with a wooden knife. It can be clearly seen that the author is experiencing difficulty in remaining fully conscious some of the time, because the handwriting left behind is extremely chaotic. There are many inadvertently engraved lines that do not belong to poetry, and also some inexplicable words. From these traces, we can infer that the poet probably inhaled hallucinogens when he wrote this poem. The particular hallucinogen used was called *akabudevelus* (the meaning of this word is "an artistic creator that causes one to hallucinate"). The process of making it was as follows: belladonna, saffron, rosemary, rosin, crocodile skin, pyroxene and some other unknown plants, animals and minerals were mashed and mixed together to produce a viscous, gelatinous substance. Then some hollow ivory was filled with cinnabar and rosewood and added to the substance. Then water was added, and it would continue to be heated after the fragrance could be smelt. Finally, it was marinated with cinnamon, pepper and sea salt. Drugs made from such a tedious process and expensive materials were extremely effective, but their effects lasted for only a short time.

The first verse of the poem describes a god who was believed not to come to the world easily, so it was called "the one who was being sought". In the first verse, the poet enthusiastically praised the god. The subsequent verses became somewhat illogical, because the potency of the hallucinogen was at its strongest at this time ("brown" probably described this hallucinogenic drug). Subsequent verses about deserts describe Timbuktu itself. The "three poets" describe a myth concerning the city's origin - three poets of a nomadic tribe went there to sacrifice their talents in exchange for water. But after describing the city, the poet wrote about the destruction of Timbuktu: "The oasis is about to die, the tower is about to fall". "Thirty days, a kingdom" describes a Moroccan myth: a great, silver-shining warrior rides his immortal steel horse, robs the world in thirty days and builds a great empire; in the end, the warrior duels with the moon and dies while devouring the moon. The poet clearly believed that the myth was true and that the soldier would come to Timbuktu and destroy the city.

[15]
In the morning
You won't be able to raise your muscles
I feel sorry for you
However
Let's go
This is the only way to live in the world

○ ○ ○   This poem was found on the northern plateau of Ethiopia and was written in Amharic. There was a very special disease spreading on this plateau. The muscles of the infected patients would dissolve slowly over three months, and eventually the whole person would lose the ability to move. According to the witch doctor, the only way to cure the disease was to go to the sea. This poem should be written by a patient to encourage his companions.

Friends from the Royal Academy of Sciences told me that the area where the disease was prevalent was far enough from the sea to turn the healthiest patient into a pool of water.

[16]

On Friday night, the moon is in the sky

The mountain lies at the centre between the wine
and the sea

I don't care about being killed

What matters is that you are no longer alive

∘ ∘ ∘　This was the slogan of Algeria's "Wine of Revenge". It was not
allowed to be displayed because it was hard to understand and violent.

[17]
You are here
Do you know?
Do not hesitate
You know
You know me
You understand us
You are one of us

Do not miss this
Do not waste it
Do not rebel
Do not resist it!

You died
Are you mocking me?

You apologize to me
You are not here
You do not know
You do not know about me
You are not soft and smooth
You are a food steamer

○ ○ ○ This poem was written in the Xhosa language. It was discovered
on a wall in a basement in Cape Town, South Africa.

[18]
Hello
You are one of us
In the trunk
Around me
This is one
What are the characteristics?

∘∘∘ This poem was discovered in South Africa. It is in the Xhosa language. One day in 1962, Ms. Elizabeth, a saleswoman living in Durban, South Africa, received a telephone call. On the caller's side there was a voice murmuring the poem, with a slight tremor in the background. After many unsuccessful attempts at identifying the caller, Ms. Elizabeth hung up. Five days later, her body was found in the trunk of a car. The cause of death was the heat.

[19]
Eternally alive
It is a kind of loneliness
It burns itself
It wants to die:
This is my dream
Death
Is that so?
One moment please
I am one of you
You are a lonely island
You are the ruler of this world
You are the eternal man
Here you are ——
My death!

○ ○ ○   This poem was written in Swahili. It was found on the walls of
an abandoned palace, written in human blood. My guide said that the
original handwriting reflected "great pain". There were many bones
beneath the walls. It is worth noting that all the skulls had a scar that
went from the left eyebrow to the right jaw. The guide said it might
be a ritual for the deceased, to achieve a certain effect that only God
knows.

[20]

The sky shone on the glass
Fascism gave four limbs
Mountains gave the body
Inherency and the contemporary age
Silence on the day of death

○ ○ ○   In 1988, while walking on the beach in Iceland with my friend, Sir Willis of Imperial College, London, I found a bottle which had been washed onto the shore. Inside was a piece of paper, with this poem written on it. The bottle also contained rose petals, coins, a black triangle and an exquisite blanket. The bottle was cracked, presumably because of high temperature. The verses in the poem were poor and incoherent. The handwriting of the first four lines was extremely sloppy, but the last line had been written with such force that it even broke the pen once.

On the back of the paper, in an ancient Egyptian dialect, the following sentences had been scribbled: "I am sorry for those innocent souls who died. I fought [illegible] for thousands of years, and only I could stop the day of death, so I had to survive. I admit it's selfish to consume a soul in order to stand up, but [illegible] above! I[illegible] another eternal winter is coming, but this time it's even worse. I failed once before, and now I cannot fail again. The book is here, so I can see how many rose petals have arrived here. Books cannot be destroyed by normal means, but pure fire can burn them... But it also means that the flame will go out [illegible handwriting, showing suffering] I have cheated Death for thousands of years... Maybe it is time to end... Maybe I will survive? But later [illegible] needs [after which the handwriting is soaked with water]."

Sir Willis said that the blanket contained patterns of Gnosticism, Buddhism and immortality. He took the black triangle and said he was going to give it to his colleagues in the physics department to study.

将·逝·之·诗

别册

将逝之诗（别册）
contents

关于《将逝之诗》

॰
॰
॰

    三个北京十一学校的国际班高二学生，在无涯学海苦渡中偶然发现了一种奇妙的文字游戏，即利用翻译软件，将自己完全不懂的语言字母随机输入，靠软件的智能联想创造出句子。经过一段时间的经验积累，竟然成功地创作出了一批优秀的诗作。

    这些诗歌风格各异，长短不一，原始文本跨越世界十几种语言。在此基础上，他们决定给每首诗歌写一段注释，其中以一些代表意象为线索，草蛇灰线地串起来了几个故事。三位学生还假造了一个作者，假托其名写下了这本书。

    该作品的主创宫梓铭自我解读："以往创作一个文学作品的过程，是先产生出一个它的'灵魂'，即内在意义或主题，随后围绕着它搭建文字，即肉体。而我们的作品，是剑走偏锋地先搭建出了文学的肉体，再创造灵魂——真正赋予这些诗歌超越于文本之上的意义的实际上是注释，而它们是在诗歌存在之后被创作出来的。我想，我们的这个尝试从某种意义上来说是一次文学实验，看看当我们写下完全不知道含义的文本后，能够怎样为它们赋予意义。"

    他们将他们的实践称之为：逆文学。

    宫梓铭：《人民文学》最年轻的作者；2019年获"北大培文杯"一等奖；曾在《萌芽》《文艺报》等报刊发表多篇作品，并出版作品集《去萨莱的路上》。

    赵文瑞：中学生独立电影制作人，作品《过气作家》获北京（国际）大学生影像展最佳中学生作品提名。

    李天翼：热爱自然科学，地质学尤甚。

写诗与"作"诗 　　　△ 黄怒波

°°°

　　阅读这本《将逝之诗》的同时，也在看斯蒂芬·金的《它》。

　　一本诗集，一本小说，没想到在读完之后才发现，它们竟殊途同归——纯属虚构。

　　斯蒂芬·金述说的故事，你在读它的第一个字起，就已知是虚构，而这本《将逝之诗》，当你认真地从第一个字读起，一直到认真地读完最后一个字，才会在"后记"中发现，它的全部内容都是虚构的。诗集的编译者——号称冰岛的古戈尔·权斯莱特，其实是"Google Translate"，至于把它的国籍归属于冰岛，只是三位真实写手们在使用谷歌翻译时发现的"冰岛语的强大"。用它"写"出来的诗句往往飘逸有仙气，意象瑰丽而深远，而且颇有些哲学意味蕴含其中。

　　是啊，难怪那些印着历史之痕，那些涂抹生命之色，那些迸发哲思之光的短诗，以及每首短诗下的细腻到充满着真实的考证元素的注解，无一不拨动着读者头脑中的理性之弦，继而轻柔地奏出冥思后的旋律。正如葡萄牙作家萨拉马戈在他的《谎言的年代》中所写道的："这短短数句诗里所表达的，远比他们第一眼瞥见时，来得丰富得多……今天若缺少了诗歌作为一种表达的管道，我们就不能称自己是完整的人。"

　　小宫同学带着他的两个小伙伴，三个十七岁的中国少年，完美地实践了创意写作，不是传统意义上的写作，是将自己的突发奇想付诸网络，由网络实施的书写。在此之前，宫梓铭出版过自己的小说访谈集《去萨莱路上》，谢冕先生曾肯定他"拥有很多同龄人所没有的探求意识、独立思想和表达能力"，这本《将逝之诗》用小宫的话来说是一次"逆文学"实验。文学，在曾经一以贯之地呐喊或是低语人类的声音之后，如今，又依托毫无人类情感和文明程度、文化积累的电子设备，用几根手指随意敲出了些许耐人寻味、引人深思的词句，诗文中涉及的宗教、宇宙、时间、生命、死亡……会诱发你对过往的追忆，对未来的畅想，对碌碌无为的懊恼，对无奈生存的力量。

这本薄薄的诗集，是对"写作"方法或是技巧的一种探索，像是文字版的"抖音"，印刷装订而成的"快手"。

这是现代性的一种吗？这是"世俗主义"的一种吗？我们该相信什么？我们能娱乐什么？我们无法超脱在时间之外，我们的内心希望哪些美好能成为永恒？在你一生所受到的善恶分两边的教导中，你仅凭一些表象而做出的评判又都是正确的吗？

原谅我的孤陋寡闻，这本诗集是我读到的第一本与其他诗人的写作手法"对立"的诗集。它的"写作"手法独特，曾经一度攫获了我的思索，更有一些诗句给我留下了强烈而隽永的记忆。

我由衷希望本书的三位年轻作者，在作品结集出版后，由此向中国原创诗歌创作出发，忠诚于自我美好情感、人间欢愉或悲凉，忠诚于诗歌的尊严。

是为序。

（△ 作者系中国诗歌学会会长、北京大学中国诗歌研究院常务副院长）

《将逝之诗》推荐

△ 姚海军

　　每个人都能感受到科学技术对我们生活的改变，但却很少有人意识到，科学技术同样正在冲击艺术的边界。在人工智能、基因编辑等领域，科学技术实际上已经成为一种艺术表达的手段。

　　《将逝之诗》中的诗作，也与科学技术有关。这体现在本书富有幻想色彩的创作过程中：三个高二学生依靠翻译软件，以自己完全不掌握的语言字母为元素，随机输入，这批诗作随即产生。如果事情到此为止，读者或许仅会将此视为一个颇具脑洞的文学玩笑，但作者并未止步于此，他们为这些诗作加上了注释，而这些释文本身又形成了另一个故事，讲述一位不存在的诗人对人类文明的发掘。

　　诗与释的互文创造出新的空间，这让本书有了文学的趣味。

（△　作者系《三体》出版人、科幻大咖）

"我的心略大于整个宇宙"

△ 小宫妈妈

——小宫和他们的"逆文学"实验

○ ○ ○

《将逝之诗》这本诗集问世了。从未想到儿子笔下会有这样的故事，过去的宫梓铭沉浸在历史里，沉醉于文学的字里行间，如今他又痴迷于宗教、神学与哲学，无中生有地创作出这本"伪书"诗集，成为妈妈艰难时光里的无比安慰。

一切的开端起始于宫梓铭与两个同学在电脑上一番穷极无聊的操作。众所周知，谷歌翻译的联想功能十分强大，可以牵强附会地将一些混乱词语转换为有意义的句子。小宫和小伙伴们便选择一门语言（往往使用拉丁字母），随后按照臆测的发音规则，一点一点地敲打出词语，看着另一边翻译过去的中文，期待着能有什么神奇的结果——

"刚开始是用斯瓦希里语，直到某一天发现冰岛语的强大。用它'写'出来的诗句往往飘逸有仙气，意象瑰丽而深远，而且颇有些哲学意味蕴含其中。"

三个北京十一学校的国际班高二学生，在无涯学海苦渡中偶然发现的这种奇妙的文字游戏，经过一段时间的经验积累，竟然成功地创作出了一批优秀的诗作。诗歌风格各异，长短不一，原始文本跨越世界十几种语言。

到这个时候，小宫们的诗歌创作还不过是消遣。直到决定将它们编写成一本"伪书"。小宫突发奇想，将这些谷歌AI诗歌，假托为冰岛诗人"古戈尔·权斯莱特"苦心孤诣寻找的"人类将逝之诗"，然后由他负责撰写大部分

< 0 0 5 >

注释，解释每首诗背后的故事，如何从世界各地收集而来，其内容颇似态度严谨的考据，实际则是无中生有的杜撰。深厚的知识积累、开阔的视野、老到高级的文字，让这些注释如此可信，以至于妈妈与那些学识渊博的朋友们都认为真有其人、真有其书、真有其事。2019年春，在IB最关键考试的最惨烈时段，三个小伙伴用旺盛的创造力表达对文学的挚爱：他们只花了一周就完成了这个作品，并将其打印出来，到学校的活动上售卖，竟然颇受欢迎。也只有在十一学校自由宽容的土壤里，才能容忍青春如此不羁地绽放。

让我们以最放松的心境，欣赏这青春的创造：

和尚的灯

打开蓝色极地冰

它是真正的火花

在夜晚闪耀

小宫在注释中这样写道：

这首诗来自冰岛西北最寒冷的地区，因此使得其中对"和尚"的描述显得有些奇怪。众所周知，冰岛之前信奉诺德信仰，后来转成基督教，几乎从未与佛教进行接触。我在当地寻求帮助的时候，遇到了一位历史学家伊瓦尔先生，我们经过讨论后理清了这么一条线索：在蒙古人西征的时候，有大量蒙古后裔留在了现在伏尔加河流域（现俄罗斯卡尔梅克共和国境内）。据说利斯塔·阿勃拉姆，一位来自以色列的诺斯替教派信徒，于13世纪来到了这里并定居了下来，诺斯替教与当地的泛灵信仰融合成了一种奇妙的宗教流派。后来16世纪土尔扈特人征服了这里，佛教又与之融合。

在17世纪，一位来自阿斯特拉罕（那附近的一座城市）的独眼商人，也是之前那个诺斯替信徒的后代，利斯塔·阿勃拉姆十二世，来到了冰岛，在西北方向的一座冰山旁建立了一座寺庙。当时的居民不了解其历史，便将他简单地称作"和尚"。他的一家人从此居住在了寺庙里。人们不喜欢这一家人，因为他们说话有严重的口音，且举止怪异：每一代利斯塔都会带着一个眼罩，他们解释为"家族传统"。在二战期间，据历史学家所描述，当地人目击到他的后代利斯塔·阿勃拉姆二十一世举着"橙红色的光"进入了他的寺庙，随后冰面裂开，发出淡淡的蓝光，整个寺庙消失不见，只剩下橙红色的火焰持续燃烧，昼夜不绝。我亲自到那个传说中的地址探索了一遍，甚至雇用了一位渔夫载我前往海里，尝试寻找这座寺庙的痕迹。什么都没有被发现，我唯一的收获是埋在浅海中的一块带链子的石头，石头上凹下去一个三角形的形状。这个也许是项链的东西被我收藏在家中，权当纪念。

诺贝尔文学奖得主莫言在看完这本小书后评价：这本书技术上有新意，建立在孩子们丰富的知识基础上。尽管对自己这种传统作家来讲，还缺少了什么，但他们17岁，前途无量。一向厚爱年轻人的莫言老师，欣然为这本书题写书名，以奖掖中国少年无所畏惧的勇气和才华。一些文学评论家慨叹00后们令人惊叹的创新能力，指出这些注释，所涵盖的知识内容，所体现的宏阔视野，所创造的故事意境，让人很难想象出自17岁高中生之手。

后来我知道官梓铭策划创意这本诗集，更重要的影响源于《哈扎尔辞典》，这是塞尔维亚作家米洛拉德·帕维奇的杰作，它将史诗和传说融在了一股魔鬼气质之中。在这个春天，小官和妈妈一起出去吃饭时，他总是随身带着这本书。

如同一两个月前，他爱上那位被罗素称为"天才人物的最完美范例"的哲学家维特根斯坦，吃饭的时候也是总带着那本斯坦福大学教授写的厚厚的传记。爱书的孩子啊，尽管吃饭的时候根本没有多少空余的时间看书，但他与书形影不离已经成为一种习惯。我曾调笑他的偶像们跟着他到海底捞涮羊肉，到徽商小馆吃臭鲑鱼，到家门口小店品小炒口蘑，享尽21世纪的人间味道。不久前去香港看我的日子，他带来的那本马基雅维利的《君主论》，应该也在西贡码头沾染过大海的湿润。感谢我的孩子将我的视野拉入无比辽远的世界。跟着他，那个未名湖畔抄录过一整本诗歌的文学青年，重新走入文学殿堂。充满好奇与激情的自我探索，也让他自己的世界变大了。文学、书籍代表着延展到很远的世界，那是更加开阔的地平线，从那里折回源于各种世代的声音，那些人类历史上最为宝贵丰富的思想，足以穿透习以为常的生活。

当然，对宫梓铭而言，所有的阅读都是对世界丰富性的体验，在文学或史学、哲学的王国里，他是一个幸福的漫游者，全然没有现实世界的包袱。佩索阿说，"我的心略大于整个宇宙"。如果说每一位写作者都有一个构建新世界的雄心，那么《将逝之诗》让人们看到小宫们的"新世界"，这里有孟加拉湾湿热的海风、月光照耀的落叶，地点可能是阿斯特拉罕城郊一家旅店、古老丹麦北部的海滩、法国尼斯的萨雷雅集市、伟大的庞贝古城、奥古斯都的德国城堡、尼禄统治下的永恒之城罗马、西班牙科尔多瓦的宫殿、非洲南部的德拉肯斯山脉、高棉王国的壮美之城吴哥窟，以及毫无防范的阿尔及利亚。

故事还可能是蒙古人的西征，诺斯替教派超自然的学说，维京海盗与印第安人的恩怨，纳粹德国的领袖意志，古代腓尼基文难以辨识的宗教符号，列支敦士登的隐秘建筑师组织，一首乌拉尔山石壁上漫漶的斯拉夫诗歌，一段肯尼亚海岸某村庄朽烂的当地木雕，一株埃塞俄比亚东南的沙漠河谷中的参天大树，一座俄罗斯阿斯特拉罕的东正教堂，一位善于写作的虚无主义哲学家，一些没有杂质、仿佛纯粹的火焰一般的巨大星体，或是一位热爱风琴的中世纪贵族。

> 大海在岛上飞行
> 月亮变成了白宫
> 没有故事的洞穴
> 充满闪电的山峰

你看看周围的镜子

这是噩梦般的粉红色

在我面前的人是精神焕发的

他在我面前疯狂

他没有生气

相反，这是一位孤独的圣人

如果不是作者揭秘，这首看似语无伦次的诗，真像4世纪的宗教呓语。《将逝之诗》中，很多类似诗句及其解释让人不明觉厉，带着原始的神秘，以及古老的敌意，让人充满敬畏，颇能体现作者的知识功力。在煞有其事地讲了一段"寻诗"故事之后，小宫用老练的笔调写着：

    有意思的是，这一希腊文作品，被发现于一根石柱上。石柱的另一边有几句对于这位先知的描写，原文如下：

    "他衣衫褴褛，瘦骨嶙峋，无法行走；但是他的眼睛 —— 哦！他的眼睛是如此的深邃，令人难以捉摸，仿佛在凝视着海底的深渊一般……可能那就是为什么他只有一只眼睛的原因，伟大的诸神无法忍受有一双这样的眼睛……"

    这段描写的下方，有另外一句话：

    "我自由了"

搭建一个文学作品的过程，是先产生出一个它的"灵魂"，即内在意义或主题，随后围绕着它搭建文字，即肉体。而小宫们的作品，是剑走偏锋地先搭建出了文学的肉体，再创造灵魂——真正赋予这些诗歌超越于文本之上的意义的实际上是注释，而它们是在诗歌存在之后被创作出来的。小宫自认为，可以看作是一种"逆文学"，一次文学实验，看看当写下完全不知道含义的文本后，能够怎样为它们赋予意义。

那个时候，我们的城市

在黑暗中驾驭，越陷越深

它有灰铁和雾的色调

伟大的上帝烧毁了月亮

这一天立刻落入旋涡之中

一会儿，它变得黑暗而无形

然后他落到了夜晚

落到了他晚安的睡眠当中

如果不看注释，你会如何理解这首诗？小宫的笔下是如此诠释的：

高棉王国的伟大都城吴哥窟在15世纪开始衰败，从一个区域性的大都市演变成了丛林中废弃的遗迹。这首用古高棉语写成的诗被发现于吴哥窟的一尊佛像上，是被粗鲁地用金属刻上去的。这尊佛像的位置比较偏僻，我敢相信除了我之外没有别的人在最近的几十年内到达过这里，这些美丽的雕像都开始生锈了。佛像旁边的石墙上刻着一些文字，大约是居民们控诉整个天空正在消失，太阳和月亮在隐没，黑暗笼罩了这座城市：他们不得不离开这个地方。这与历史上的记载比较吻合，吴哥并不是一瞬间衰败的，而是经历了一个漫长的过程。

宫梓铭告诉我，《将逝之诗》里面很多注释是相互有关联的，它们串成了三个故事。惭愧的是，我还没有解读出来。愚钝如我，连一个旅人在冬夜也看不懂的我，如何能理解他的世界？只能直观地感受，他以心灵的脚步跨越了整个宇宙。正如他自己在伪托的《巴黎文学》评论中所言："这部作品已经远远超越了'诗集'这一体裁的限制，它揭示了世界不为人知的一角，让读者意

< 010 >

识到人类的伟大"。

　　　　垂悬在山脉的黑月亮
　　　　发出惊人的红光
　　　　风在树林里说话
　　　　我不知道那种语言是什么

　　　　蓝色的乌鸦带来了他的信件
　　　　蜡和泡沫深绿茶纸
　　　　扭曲的笔触和奇怪的线条
　　　　我不知道那种语言是什么

　　　　他不可能在那里
　　　　远在沙漠中的古庙
　　　　沙子将风吹过
　　　　我不知道那种语言是什么

　　就诗歌表现力而言，这些AI诗句给人一种眩晕的美感，虽然我更喜欢那些充满想象和勇气的注释，但这本书中的诗句，同样是值得一读的，它们瑰丽的意象和深刻的寓意，甚至并不逊色于里尔克的"我认出风暴而激动如大海"。

　　"人类就像在沙滩上奔跑的孩子，而文字就是他的脚印。孩子跑向远方的同时，他的脚印正在被抹除。我所做的，无非是建造一座沙做的大坝，暂时守护那一点属于过去的脚印，为孩子勾勒出他的旅程……"

　　这是孩子们假托大师之口写的一段话，我特别喜欢。天才的编辑麦克斯帕金斯说过，一本模仿别人的书永远低人一等。但三个17岁孩子模仿中的创造，是否也是一种电光石火的天赋？

诗集中有一首诗，为许多读者所喜爱，内容是这样的：

有时一本书静静地睡着了

风轻轻地呼吸着空气

它将慢慢打开花瓣和眼睑，如威尼斯玫瑰

但他们看不到任何东西

木星蓝色的灵魂像天鹅绒一样柔软

有时在阳光下度过一整天的精华

每一朵云都有自己的竖琴

在高云边缘闪耀的颜色

人们对这令人印象深刻的光芒感到惊讶

他们闭着眼睛

严肃地凝视着

阳光在海上爆发

火炮，烟花和火药！

然后今晚湍流的光线平静下来

地平线将是圆的，美丽的，蓝色的

在里面，它包含了世界的闪闪发光的全景

但是，死岛永远不会复活

这就是生命的意义

你能想象小宫们如何赋予这首诗以生命吗？他们会怎样叙述与诠释，又会如何在广袤的世界、历史的天空里，驰骋自己天马行空的想象？

答案即将呈现。如不出意外，《将逝之诗》将由四川人民出版社出版。更多读者能从中得窥中国少年无拘无束的青春牧场，那是时代给予他们的恩宠，是北京十一学校美丽校园里的青春往事。

亲爱的孩子们，愿你们毫无负担的奔跑，愿每一点沙土都令你们欢愉。

（△　作者系主创宫梓铭的妈妈）

后记

△ 宫梓铭

　　一切的开端起始于赵文瑞与我在电脑上一番穷极无聊的操作。众所周知，谷歌翻译的联想功能十分强大，可以牵强附会地将一些混乱词语转换为有意义的句子。我们便选择一门语言（往往使用拉丁字母），随后按照我们臆测的发音规则，一点一点地敲打出词语，看着另一边翻译过去的中文，期待着能有什么神奇的结果。这样，我们丝毫不知道自己在写什么，但也能够产生句子。起初，翻译的结果非常简单幼稚，不过是一些略显荒诞的句子罢了。后来经过一番努力，我们掌握了一些规律，成功地"写"出了连贯的诗句。

　　刚开始是用斯瓦希里语，因为不管多么看似不符合常理的字母排布，谷歌翻译都能将它转换为诗句。书中非洲组诗大部分与"珍珠"相关的诗歌均是这个时代的作品。后来我们零零碎碎地创作，拖了很久，直到某一天发现冰岛语的强大。用它"写"出来的诗句往往飘逸有仙气，意象瑰丽而深远，而且颇有些哲学意味蕴含其中。于是第二次创作高峰开始了。

　　到这个时候，我们的诗歌创作还不过是消遣。直到我们决定将它们编写成一本书籍。我由《哈扎尔词典》的体裁中获得灵感，认为创作一本"伪书"是很好的选择。加之里面很多诗歌有奇妙的共通的名词或剧情，将其串成一个庞大的、统一的故事是一个很好的选择。于是我们开始了创作。起初只有我和赵文瑞两个人，后来又加入了李天翼。我主要负责编写大部分注释，赵文瑞负责将这本书伪造得更惟妙惟肖，设计了封面，修改了排版等；他与李天翼也编写了一些注释。我们共花了一周就完成了这个作品，将其打印出来，到学校的活动上售卖。

也是在这个时候，我意识到了这本书更加深层的意义。它不仅仅是一个为了好玩的消遣，也不仅仅是含有幽默成分在内的行为艺术，而是某种更加深奥的事物。书中的诗歌各有其风格，也不乏出彩的词句，但要论功行赏，谁是它们的作者呢？显然不是谷歌翻译，它只是一个工具；但也不是我们，因为我们也不知道自己所敲打下的字母能够给诗句带来怎样的变化。这可以被看作是一个"逆文学"了。搭建一个文学作品的过程，是先产生出一个它的"灵魂"，即内在意义或主题，随后围绕着它搭建文字，即肉体。而我们的作品，是剑走偏锋地先搭建出了文学的肉体，再创造灵魂——真正赋予这些诗歌超越于文本之上的意义的实际上是注释，而它们是在诗歌存在之后被创作出来的。我想，我们的这个尝试从某种意义上来说是一次文学实验，看看当我们写下完全不知道含义的文本后，能够怎样为它们赋予意义。我想，这也是这本书的意义了。

古戈尔·权斯莱特的原稿

翻译   关闭即时翻译

中文　南非科萨语　拉丁语　检测语言　▼   ⇄   僧伽罗语　中文(简体)　南非科萨语　▼   翻译

we lu pi sa mo ku la   ✕   我们在这个页面上阅读它
ha mu so li pi so wa   它不在你的心中
ba wi ci to fu li to   他们必须这样做
bu ni mo wa qua   这是一个要求
                                      78/5000   📋 🔊   ✎ 提出修改建议

中文　南非科萨语　斯瓦希里语　检测语言　▼   ⇄   英语　中文(简体)　南非科萨语　▼   翻译

unguasi lazi   ✕   你在这里
ung uas il azi   你知道吗?
ung uasil azi   不要犹豫
unguasilazi.   你知道的。
u nguasilazi   你认识我
u nguasilazi   你了解我们
unguasi la zi   你是其中之一

ung ua si la zi   不要错过这个
ung ua silazi   不要浪费
ung uasi lazi,   不要反叛,
ung uasi lazi!   不要反抗它!

ung uasila zi,   你死了,
ung uasilaz i   你在嘲笑我吗?
unguasilaz i   你对我很抱歉
unguasil a zi   你不在这里
ungu asilazi   你不知道
ungu asilaz i   你不知道我
u ngua silazi   你并不柔滑
u nguasi lazi   你是一个蒸笼
🔊   268/5000   📋 🔊   ✎ 提出修改建议

< 　018　 >

O ma ke kai e lele ma luna o mokupuni

Ua lilo ka mahina a lil'o i hale keokeo

cave lai i ka moolelo olelo ka

o ka mauna maona luna ka uila

O wo lilami wawa o lika

O po lilami wawa o lika

Mai ole e luma bok hoomaha

O do lilami wawa o li'ka

aoleo ia hehena

o lane saioka kama si

大海在岛上飞行

月亮变成了白宫

没有故事的洞穴

充满闪电的山峰

你看看周围的镜子

这是噩梦般的粉红色

在我面前的人是精神焕发的

他在我面前疯狂

他没有生气

相反，这是一个孤独的圣人

<Að læra svokölluð tungumál>

Ég man í morgun
glær morgun
Ég er að keyra á bak við nokkur börn
Undir fótunum eru mjúkir jarðvegur og gras sem dansar í vindi
Sólin virtist vera eins og blíður litur á okkur
Við erum að, eins og lömb við ánni
við komum í dilapidated musteri
Ég sá nokkra stóra guði
Það virðist vera í gangi í langan tíma
Hins vegar eru þeir að deyja

Það var kvöld, stormur fór bara.
Myrkur skýin á himni eru eins og rúllandi reykur
Ég sit við tjörnina að baki húsinu, í blautum landslagi
Undarlega maður kom til mín
Hann er með svört föt
Eins svartur fáninn flutti undir myrkrinu himni
Hann sagði að ég ætti að fara á þessum degi
Sérstök dagur í þessu óendanlegu alheimi

<学习所谓的语言>

我记得今天早上
明媚的早晨
我跑在一些孩子身后
脚下是柔软的土壤和草地，在风中跳舞
太阳似乎对我们来说就像一种温柔的色彩
我们就像河边的羔羊一样
我们来到一个破旧的寺庙
我看到了一些伟大的神灵
这似乎已经持续了很长时间
然而，他们正在死去

那天晚上，暴风雨刚过去了。
天空中的乌云像滚滚的烟雾
我坐在房子后面的池塘里，在潮湿的风景中
一个陌生的男人来找我
他有黑色的衣服
随着黑旗在黑暗的天空下移动
他说我应该继续这一天
这个无限宇宙中的特殊日子

| 拉丁语 | 挪威语 | 世界语 | 检测语言 | ∨ | | ⇄ | 宿务语 | 中文(简体) | 中文(繁体) | | 翻译 |

do kvo
ado kvo
as do kvo
asf do kvo
asfa do kvo
asfaa do kvo
asfaat do kvo
asfaaty do kvo
asfaatyb do kvo

太热了
我爱水
这么多水
那是多么的热
沥青为水
渴望水
让我们拿到你的水
把你的水倒掉
我要去喝水

105/5000

| 检测语言 | 中文 | 蒙古语 | 冰岛语 | ∨ | | ⇄ | 蒙古语 | 中文(简体) | 冰岛语 |

цүргубу хйшоунш яйшршйнш
яхуёш цүнү иазши яхургхгй буш айшншай:
чшйи яйш нш ршиа чшу цйи лшйиа бгйи лу!
ойифшлйш яхунйиабу ёхүиаауиалс айүншчшу

цүчшхгйи эшйиагүяхшцйиа бйиыхш яуиту нүиаыхйаях ургхгй
яхуршйиаыхш ягшхү гншргхгй цүчшцйиаэйхуи ишгмш
яху ыхүгыхшойи фшлйшхйү чшйиа агйинг йшн гы шцйиа
цү ршучшй лйшчг нйү яйшчшу рш рг хгй?

ыхйиа ёш цү нүиа ншиацуи
ыхуш рг гу мшйи бу ауиа нүг нш ыш лу
хйш нүг ягшхүг ншбгйи нйучшу яхуи ыхшмгжүиа нш
яхуёш ыхшяхуияхуиабу ягшхүг ншргхгй лу

цушбуыхш жйиа яхуыхүгыхш ауиарш ыхгиёхйиа
цүнйү ёхүиачшичшу яхургхгйь чшцйиа мгёгп
цү чшхгйи яхуту чшуыхшь яхуи бу
жйихүгмй ыхшрг ёх үиач ши зйшлшу ыхгичг

冬天的匆忙
几乎无法预测:
她是一个利维亚人!
欢迎来到爱的世界

不可预知的预言
顽固的不朽之隙
天国之王
你不觉得自己是统治者吗?

你是诅咒你的人
你可以隐藏罪恶
死亡之罪是真理
你不能只是隐藏它

不管你的生活是什么
你不想打破你的怀抱
为什么不呢?
你知道怎样毁了你的生活

Vanishing Poems (Annexe)
Contents

About *Vanishing Poems*

○
○
○

Three Grade 11 students from the international class at Beijing National Day School, in their endless quest of knowledge, stumbled upon an amazing word game. This game involved using translation software to randomly input the letters of a language they did not know at all, and to create sentences by using the intelligence of the software. After a period of accumulating experience with this method, a number of excellent poems were successfully created.

This involved different poetic styles and different length, and the original texts of them from across the world were written in more than a dozen languages. On this basis, they decided to write an explanatory note for each poem, in which some representative images were used as clues to string together several stories. So the three students also faked an author and composed the book in his name.

Gong Ziming, the creators of this work, explains: "The process of building a literary work in the past was to first produce its 'soul', i.e. its internal meaning or theme, and then build a text, i.e. the body, around it. But our work deviates from the norm by first building the body of a poem and then creating the soul. What really gives these poems meaning beyond themselves is in fact the annotations, which were created after the poems. I think our attempt is, in a sense, a literary experiment, to see how we can give meaning to texts when we write them without knowing the background meaning at all."

They call their method "anti-literature".

Gong Ziming: writing enthusiast, winner of the first prize of the Peiwen Cup Competition held by Peking University in 2019; the youngest author to have published an article in the magazine *People's Literature*; author of many articles in *Meng Ya, Literature and Art Newspaper* and other periodicals, as well as a collection of works entitled *On the Way to Salai*.

Zhao Wenrui: middle school student, independent filmmaker, whose work *An Outdated Writer* has been nominated for the Best Middle School Student Production Award at the Beijing (International) College Student Video Exhibition.

Li Tianyi: student, with an ardent love for natural sciences, especially geology.

Writing and "Creating" Poetry

o o o

While reading the book *Vanishing Poems*, I also read Stephen King's *It*.

One is a collection of poems, the other, a novel. I did not expect to discover after reading them that they both had the same goal, but reached it by different means. The goal was that of pure fiction. One realizes from the very first word that the story told by Stephen King is fiction. But *Vanishing Poems* does not reveal its fictionality until you read the final words of the appendices. The compiler of the poems, Gúg. l Tríntl.t of Iceland, is actually "Google Translate". As for attributing his nationality to Iceland, it was when using Google Translate that three real writers discovered the "power of the Icelandic language". The poems "written" in this language are often elegant and magical, with magnificent and profound images, and quite a few philosophical implications.

Indeed, no wonder that these short poems with traces of history, the colour of life, the light of philosophical thought, and the exquisite explanation full of elements of authentic textual research under each short poem, all touch a chord of rationality in the reader's mind, and then play a gentle melody of meditation. As the Portuguese writer Saramago wrote in his book *The Age of Lies*: "The expression in these short poems is much richer than your first glimpse of them… Today, without poetry as a channel of expression, one cannot call oneself a complete person. "

Xiao Gong and his two young friends, three seventeen-year-old Chinese teenagers, have perfectly refined creative writing, not writing in the traditional sense, but have input their sudden whims onto the Internet and the Internet executed their writing. Prior to that, Gong Ziming had published his own collection of fictional interviews, *On the Way to Salai*. Mr. Xie Mian affirmed that he had "a sense of exploration, independent thinking and an expressive ability that many of his peers did not have." This anthology, *Vanishing Poems*, in the words of Xiao Gong, is an experiment in "anti-literature". Literature, having shouted or whispered using human voices, now, relying on electronic devices without human emotions, civilizations or cultural accumulation, taps out some interesting and thought-provoking words at will, through the use of a few fingers. The poems touch on religion, the universe, time, life, and death… They will induce you to recall the past, imagine the future, regret inaction, and find the strength to face helplessness.

This thin collection of poems is an exploration of "writing" methods or techniques. It is like a literary form of the Douyin (抖音, Tik Tok in English) app, or the Kuaishou (快手, literally translated as "deft hand") app in printing and binding.

Is this a kind of modernity? Is this a kind of "secularism"? What should we believe? What can we turn into entertainment? Since we cannot transcend time, what good things would our hearts desire to be eternal? Are we right to judge only by appearances according to the teaching of good and evil in our lives?

Forgive my ignorance. This collection of poems is the first one I have ever read that "contradicts" the writing techniques of other poets. Its "writing" technique is unique, and once made me think a lot. There are also some poems that left me with strong and meaningful memories.

I sincerely hope that the three young authors of this book, after the publication of their work, will proceed to the creation of original Chinese poetry and be loyal to their personal good feelings, to the joy and sorrow of ordinary people, and to the dignity of poetry.

I hereby present this article as a preface.

(△ This preface is written by Huang Nubo, the president of the Chinese Poetry Society and the executive vice-president of the Chinese Poetry Academy of Peking University.)

Recommendation for *Vanishing Poems*
○ ○ ○

Everybody has experienced the transformation that science and technology have brought to our lives, but there are only a few people who have realized that science and technology are also having an impact on the boundaries of art. In the fields of artificial intelligence and gene editing, science and technology have in fact become a means of artistic expression.

The poems in the anthology *Vanishing Poems* are also related to science and technology. This is reflected in the amazing creative process of this book: three Grade 11 students used translation software to randomly input letters of a language which they did not know at all, and then the poems in this book were produced. If this were the end of the story, the reader would most probably consider it to be a profound literary joke, but the authors did not stop there. They added annotations to these poems, which in turn have become another story about the unearthing of human civilization by a non-existent poet.

The connections they establish between the poems and their explanations create a new domain, which enables the book to convey its own literary insight.

(⊿　This preface is written by Yao Haijun, a well-known science fiction publisher who has published *The Three-Body Problem*.)

"My Heart Is A little Larger Than the Entire Universe"
—Xiao Gong and His Friends and Their "Literary Experiment"
∘ ∘ ∘

Vanishing Poems has finally been published. I never imagined that my son would write such a story. In the past, Gong Ziming was immersed in history and literature, but now he is obsessed with religion, theology and philosophy. The creating of this "fake book" of poems out of nothing has become a great comfort for me in my difficult times.

It all started with Gong Ziming and his two classmates carrying out extremely boring computer operations. As we all know, the association function of Google Translate is so powerful that it can transform confusing words into meaningful sentences. Xiao Gong and his friends chose a language (often using Latin letters), then typed out the words bit by bit according to speculative pronunciation rules, and looked the Chinese translations of these words, expecting magical results:

"At first the language they used was Swahili, until one day they discovered the power of Icelandic. The poems written in this language were often elegant and magical, with magnificent and profound images, and quite a few philosophical implications."

Three Grade 11 students from the international class of Beijing National Day School, who stumbled upon this wonderful word game in their endless pursuit of learning, have successfully created a number of excellent poems after a period of accumulating experience with this method. There are different poetic styles, the length of each poem is different, and the original texts cover more than a dozen languages across the world.

At this time, the composing of poems was just a pastime for Xiao Gong and his friends. Things began to change when they took the decision to transform them into a "fake" book.

Xiao Gong suddenly had an original idea - these Google AI poems should be "poems that are about to die" that an Icelandic poet, "Gúg. l Tríntl.t" had been searching for. He then wrote most of the notes explaining how the poem had been collected from all over the world. The content and style of these notes is similar to that of rigorous textual research, but in fact it is pure fiction. These notes are so credible because of their breadth of knowledge, broad vision and advanced writing style, that I and my knowledgeable friends all thought that they related to real people, books and facts. In the spring of 2019, at the height of the International Baccalaureate's most critical exam, these three young students expressed their love for literature by making use of their extraordinary creativity. It took them only a week to complete the work, print it out and sell it at school events, and it was very popular. Only in the free and open-minded atmosphere of Beijing National Day School could such an uninhibited burgeoning of young minds be allowed to flourish.

Let us appreciate the creativity of these young minds in a relaxed manner:

The monk's lamp

Sheds forth blue polar ice

It is a genuine flame

Shining in the night

Xiao Gong, in his explanatory notes, writes:

This poem comes from the coldest part of Northwest Iceland. Therefore, it makes the description of the "monk" seem somewhat strange. As is well known, Icelandic people originally believed in the Nordic religion and only later converted to Christianity. They hardly ever came in contact with Buddhism. When I asked people in that area for help in understanding, I met a historian named Mr. Ivar, and after discussion, we came up with the following chain of events: during the Mongolian Western Expedition, a large number of Mongolian descendants remained in the Volga River Basin (now in the territory of the Republic of Kalmyk, Russia). It is said that Lista Abram, a Gnostic believer from Israel, arrived in this area in the thirteenth century and settled here. Mongolians believe in immortality, and their pantheistic belief coincided with the Gnostic supernatural doctrine and the two religions fused into an intriguing belief system. Later, in the sixteenth century, the Tuerhute ethnic group conquered the area, and Buddhism merged with the local religion.

In the seventeenth century, a one-eyed businessman from Astrakhan, a nearby city, also a descendant of the Gnostic believer, Lista Abram of the twelfth generation, came to Iceland and a temple

< 0 3 1 >

was built near an iceberg in the northwest part of the country. The inhabitants at that time did not know his own history and simply called him a "monk". His family lived in a temple ever since that time. People did not like the family because they spoke with a heavy accent and displayed unusual behaviour. Every generation of Lista wears eyeshades, because it is a tradition in their family clan.

During the Second World War, local people witnessed one descendant, Lista Abram of the twenty-first generation, enter his temple with an "orange-red light", then the ice cracked, giving off a faint blue light. Subsequently the whole temple disappeared, leaving only the orange-red flame which burnt day and night. I have personally explored the legendary location and even hired a fisherman to take me out to sea, to try and find traces of the temple. I made no discovery other than a stone to which a chain was attached, buried in the sand under a shallow part of the sea. On top of the stone was a hollowed-out part in the shape of a triangle. This, perhaps, was a necklace, and I keep it at home as a souvenir.

Nobel Prize winner, Mo Yan, commented after reading this small book that it is technically innovative and based on the rich knowledge of the youngsters. Despite what traditional writers such as myself would deem to be missing in the book, these young people are only seventeen years old and have great prospects. Mr. Mo Yan, who has always been very concerned with the growth of young people, was glad to inscribe the title of this book, to reward the courage and talent of these fearless young Chinese people. Some literary critics have also noticed the amazing innovative ability of young people born after the year 2000,

< 0 3 2 >

pointing out that the annotations, the knowledge they cover, the broad vision they embody, and the artistic conception they create, make it difficult to imagine that they came from the hands of seventeen-year-old high school students.

Later I realized that when he was planning this collection of poems, the greatest influence came from *Dictionary of the Khazars*. This is the masterpiece of Serbian writer, Milorad Pavich, who blends epic and legend in his work and thus gives it a devil's temperament. During the spring, whenever Xiao Gong went out to dinner with his mother, he always took the book with him.

Just like a month or two ago, he fell in love with Wittgenstein, a philosopher whom Bertrand Russell called "the perfect example of a genius", and always had a thick biography written by a Stanford professor at dinner. As a child who loves books, even though there is not much spare time for him to read at mealtimes, he still does not want to be separated from books.

I used to make fun of his idols who followed him to the Haidilao hot-pot restaurant, to the Weishang Xiaoguan to eat fermented trout, to a small restaurant near our house to eat fried mushrooms, to taste the flavours enjoyed by people of the twenty-first century. The copy of Machiavelli's *The Prince* he brought with him when he recently visited me in Hong Kong must have been moistened by the humid sea air at the Sai Kung Pier. I thank my child for extending my horizons to an unparalleled far-reaching world. In his wake, the young literary woman who transcribed a whole poem by the nameless lake re-entered the great hall of literature. Literature and books represent a far-reaching world, a wider horizon from which the voices of generations can be retraced. The most precious and rich ideas in human history can penetrate daily life.

Of course, for Gong Ziming, all that he reads gives him an experience of the richness of the world. He is a happy wanderer in the realms of literature, history and philosophy, without any burden from the real world. Pessoa said, "My heart is a little larger than the entire universe." If every writer has an ambition to build a new world, then, *Vanishing Poems* lets people see the "new world" of Xiao Gong and his friends. There is the hot and humid sea breeze of the Bay of Bengal; the fallen leaves illuminated by the light of the moon, outside an inn on the outskirts of Astrakhan; a beach in the northern part of ancient Denmark; and the Saleya Fair in Nice, France; the great ancient city of Pompeii; the German castle that belonged to Augustus; the eternal city of Rome under Nero's rule; the palace of Cordoba in Spain; the Drakensburg Mountains of South Africa; the magnificent capital of the Khmer Kingdom, Angkor; and an Algeria caught off guard.

It may also be the Mongolian march to the West; the Gnostic supernatural doctrine; the vendetta between Viking pirates and native Indians; the will of the leaders of Nazi Germany; the indescribable religious symbols of ancient Phoenicia; a secret organization of architects in Liechtenstein; a Slavic poem written on a stone wall in the Ural Mountains; a rotting local woodcarving in a village on the coast of Kenya; a towering tree in the desert valley of southeastern Ethiopia; an Orthodox church in Astrakhan, Russia; a nihilistic philosopher who is good at writing; giant stars that are without impurities and like pure flames; or a medieval aristocrat who loved the organ.

The sea splashes over the island

The moon becomes a white palace

The caves have no stories

The mountain peaks are bathed in lightning

Look at the mirrors around you

They are the pink colour of a nightmare

He that goes ahead of me is in high spirits

He is acting in an insane manner

He is not angry

On the contrary, he is a lonely saint

Were it not for the author's explanation, this seemingly incoherent poem in fact resembles the religious language of the fourth century. Many similar poems and their explanations in *Vanishing Poems* are difficult to understand and yet powerful. They contain both primeval mystery and ancient hostility, which reflect the author's knowledge and skills and solicit the reader's admiration. After recounting a story of "poem hunting", Xiao Gong writes in an experienced style:

Interestingly, on the other side of the pillar, there are several lines describing the prophet, which read as follows:

"He was dressed in rags and emaciated, unable to walk; but as for his eyes – oh! His eyes were so deep, they were unfathomable, as if gazing into the abyss of the ocean floor... maybe that is why he has only one eye, since the mighty gods could not bear to have a pair of such eyes..."

Underneath this description there is another sentence:

"I am free".

The process of building a literary work is to first produce its "soul", that is, its meaning or theme, and then build a text around it, that is, its "body". But in Xiao Gong's works, he goes about it in a contrary fashion: first building the "body" of a work of literature and then creating its "soul". The annotations actually give the poems meaning, but they are created after the poems are written. Xiao Gong thinks that it can be considered as a kind of "anti-literature", a literary experiment, to see whether giving meaning to texts after they are written can work.

> At that time, our city
>
> Was riding in darkness, sinking deeper and deeper
>
> It had the colours of gray iron and fog
>
> The great God burned up the moon
>
> And the day immediately fell into a whirlpool
>
> After a while, it became dark and invisible
>
> Then he fell into the night
>
> He fell into his good night sleep

If you did not look at the annotation, how would you understand the poem? Xiao Gong interpreted it in this way:

> Angkor, the great capital of the Khmer Kingdom, began to decline in the fifteenth century, deteriorating from a regional metropolis to an abandoned relic in the jungle. The poem, written in ancient Khmer, was found on a statue of Buddha in Angkor Wat, roughly carved with certain metallic tools. This Buddha statue is in a

relatively remote location. I could well believe that no one else except for myself has been here in recent decades. These beautiful statues are beginning to rust. On the stone wall next to the Buddha statue are inscriptions by local inhabitants complaining that the whole sky was disappearing, that the sun and moon were invisible, and that darkness was enveloping the city: they had to leave the place. This is consistent with historical records. Angkor did not decline in an instant, but over a long period of time.

Gong Ziming told me that many of the annotations in *Vanishing Poems* are related to each other, and they form three stories. The embarrassing thing is that I did not figure that out when I was reading the poems. Slow-witted as I am, unable to recognize one single traveler on a winter's night, how can I understand his world? I can only intuitively feel that he traversed the whole universe with the footsteps of his soul. Just as he put it in his review for the fictitious *Paris Literature:* "This work has gone far beyond the limitations of the poetry anthology genre. It reveals an unknown part of the world and makes readers aware of the greatness of human beings."

The black moon hanging over the mountains
Radiates an astonishing red light
The wind is speaking in the woods
I do not know what that language is

The blue crow brought his letter
On dark green tea paper of wax and foam

Twisted strokes and strange lines

I do not know what that language is

He cannot possibly be there

In ancient temples in the desert

Sand is blown by the wind

I do not know what the language is

I think that as far as the expressive power of poetry is concerned, these AI poems give people a dizzy aesthetic feeling. Although I prefer those imaginative and courageous notes, the poems in this book, in my opinion, are also worth reading. Their magnificent images and profound implications are not even inferior to Rilke's famous line, " I already know the storm, and I am troubled as the sea. "

Mankind is like a child running on the beach, and words are his footprints. As the child runs away, his footprints begin to be erased. All I have done is to build a dam made of sand, to temporarily keep the footprints of the past, and outline his journey for the child.

The above passage is written by Gong Ziming as coming from the mouth of a master named Stanley Marsh. I like it very much. Genius editor Max Perkins said that a book that imitates others is always an inferior one. But who can deny that the creation of three seventeen-year-olds in the form of imitation not also a flash of talent?

There is a poem in the anthology which is loved by many readers. The content is as follows:

Sometimes a book falls asleep quietly

The wind gently breathes the air

It slowly opens petals and eyelids, like the Venetian rose

But people do not see anything

The blue soul of Jupiter is as soft as velvet

Sometimes spending the best prat of a day in the sunlight

Each cloud has its own harp

Colours sparkle on the edges of the high clouds

People are astonished at this awesome light

They close their eyes

They stare earnestly

The sunshine explodes over the sea

Artillery, fireworks and dynamite!

Then tonight the turbulent light becomes calm

The horizon is round, beautiful and blue

Within, it contains the dazzling panorama of the world

But the island of the dead will never rise again

This is the meaning of life

Can you imagine how Xiao Gong and his friends brought this poem to life? How they narrated and explained, and how they let their imagination gallop in a vast world full of history?

The answer will soon appear. Barring any unforeseen circumstances, *Vanishing Poems* will be published by Sichuan People's

Publishing House. An even greater number of readers will be able to get a glimpse of the free-spirited psyche of Chinese teenagers. It is the grace and favour that the current era has granted them. And it will also become a glittering memory shared by them in the beautiful campus of Beijing National Day School.

Dear young people, may you run without any burden, and may every grain of sand make you happy.

(△　This preface is written by Gong Ziming's mother.)

Addendum

○
○
○

It all started when Zhao Wenrui and I were performing a boring computer operation. As we all know, the association function of Google Translate is so powerful that it can transform confusing words into meaningful sentences. We chose a language (often with a Latin alphabet) and then, according to our supposed pronunciation rules, typed out the words bit by bit and watched the Chinese trans lations of these words, expecting magical results. This method enabled us to produce sentences even when we had no idea what we were writing. At first, the results of these translations were very simple and naive, being only a few slightly absurd sentences. Later, after much effort, we mastered some rules and succeeded in "writing" coherent poems.

At first the language we used was Swahili, because no matter how seemingly unconventional the arrangement of letters, Google Translate was able to translate it into poetry. Most of the African poems related to "pearls" in this anthology were created at this time. Later, we carried out our creation in piecemed fashion, and things remained like this for a long time, until one day we discovered the power of Icelandic. The poems written in this language were often elegant and magical, with magnificent and profound images, and quite a few philosophical associations. So the second creation climax began.

By this time, our poetic creation was just a pastime. Things began to change when we decided to compile the poems into a book. Inspired by the genre of *Dictionary of the Khazars*, I thought it would be a good choice to create a "fake" book. In addition, as many of the poems share intriguing common nouns or plots, it could be a good choice to string them together into a huge, unified story. So we started to create. At first there were only two of us, Zhao Wenrui and myself. Then later Li Tianyi joined us. I was mainly responsible for composing most of the annotations. Zhao Wenrui was responsible for making this faked book look more real. He designed the cover, modified the typeset, and undertook some other jobs. He and Li Tianyi also wrote some annotations. It took us a week to complete the work, print it out and sell it at school events.

It was also at this time that I realized the deeper significance of the book. It is not just a fun book to divert us, it is not just a form of behavioural art which includes humour, but it is something more profound. The poems in the book have their own styles, and there are many fabulous words and phrases. But who is their author when it comes to rewarding people according to their merits and contributions? Obviously it is not Google Translate, because it is just a tool. But it is not us either, because we did not know how the letters we typed could be changed into verse. The book can be regarded as "anti-literature". The process of building a literary work is to first produce its "soul", that is, its internal meaning or theme, and then build a text around it, that is, the "body". Our work, however, deviates from the normal trend by first building the "body" of a work of literature and then creating its "soul". What really gives these poems meaning beyond the text is actually the annotations, which are created after the poems are written. Our attempt is, in a sense, a literary experiment, to see how we can give meaning to texts when we write them without knowing what they mean. I think that is what this book is all about.

(△　This addendum is written by Gong Ziming.)

Gúg.l Tríntl.t's Original Manuscript

中文　南非科萨语　拉丁语　检测语言 ▼

we lu pi sa mo ku la
ha mu so li pi so wa
ba wi ci to fu li to
bu ni mo wa qua

78/5000

僧伽罗语　中文(简体)　南非科萨语 ▼　**翻译**

我们在这个页面上阅读它
它不在你的心中
他们必须这样做
这是一个要求

✏ 提出修改建议

中文　南非科萨语　斯瓦希里语　检测语言 ▼

unguasi lazi
ung uas il azi
ung uasil azi
unguasilazi.
u nguasilazi
ung uasilazi
unguasi la zi

ung ua si la zi
ung ua silazi
ung uasi lazi,
ung uasi lazi!

ung uasila zi,
ung uasilaz i
unguasilaz i
unguasil a zi
ungu asilazi
ungu asilazi i
u ngua silazi
u nguasi lazi

268/5000

英语　中文(简体)　南非科萨语 ▼　**翻译**

你在这里
你知道吗?
不要犹豫
你知道的。
你认识我
你了解我们
你是其中之一

不要错过这个
不要浪费
不要反叛,
不要反抗它!

你死了,
你在嘲笑我吗?
你对我很抱歉
你不在这里
你不知道
你不知道我
你并不柔滑
你是一个蒸笼

✏ 提出修改建议

O ma ke kai e lele ma luna o mokupuni	大海在岛上飞行
Ua lilo ka mahina a lil'o i hale keokeo	月亮变成了白宫
cave lai i ka moolelo olelo ka	没有故事的洞穴
o ka mauna maona luna ka uila	充满闪电的山峰
O wo lilami wawa o lika	你看看周围的镜子
O po lilami wawa o lika	这是噩梦般的粉红色
Mai ole e luma bok hoomaha	在我面前的人是精神焕发的
O do lilami wawa o li'ka	他在我面前疯狂
aoleo ia hehena	他没有生气
o lane saioka kama si	相反，这是一个孤独的圣人

<Að læra svokölluð tungumál>	<学习所谓的语言>
Ég man í morgun	我记得今天早上
glær morgun	明媚的早晨
Ég er að keyra á bak við nokkur börn	我跑在一些孩子身后
Undir fótunum eru mjúkir jarðvegur og gras sem dansar í vindi	脚下是柔软的土壤和草地，在风中跳舞
Sólin virtist vera eins og blíður litur á okkur	太阳似乎对我们来说就像一种温柔的色彩
Við erum að, eins og lömb við ánni	我们就像河边的羔羊一样
við komum í dilapidated musteri	我们来到一个破旧的寺庙
Ég sá nokkra stóra guði	我看到了一些伟大的神灵
Það virðist vera í gangi í langan tíma	这似乎已经持续了很长时间
Hins vegar eru þeir að deyja	然而，他们正在死去
Það var kvöld, stormur fór bara.	那天晚上，暴风雨刚过去了。
Myrkur skýin á himni eru eins og rúllandi reykur	天空中的乌云像滚滚的烟雾
Ég sit við tjörnina að baki húsinu, í blautum landslagi	我坐在房子后面的池塘里，在潮湿的风景中
Undarlega maður kom til mín	一个陌生的男人来找我
Hann er með svört föt	他有黑色的衣服
Eins svartur fáninn flutti undir myrkrinu himni	随着黑旗在黑暗的天空下移动
Hann sagði að ég ætti að fara á þessum degi	他说我应该继续这一天
Sérstök dagur í þessu óendanlegu alheimi	这个无限宇宙中的特殊日子

拉丁语　挪威语　世界语　检测语言　▾

语务语　中文(简体)　中文(繁体)　▾　　**翻译**

do kvo
ado kvo
as do kvo
asf do kvo
asfa do kvo
asfaa do kvo
asfaat do kvo
asfaaty do kvo
asfaatyb do kvo

🔊　　　　　　　　　　　　　　　　105/5000

太热了
我爱水
这么多水
那是多么的热
沥青为水
渴望水
让我们拿到你的水
把你的水倒掉
我要去喝水

📋 🔊　　　　　　　　　　　　✏ 提出修改建议

检测语言　中文　**蒙古语**　冰岛语　⌄

⇄　蒙古语　**中文(简体)**　冰岛语

цүргубу хйшоунш яйшршйнш
яхуёш цүнү иазши яхургхгй буш айшншай:
чшйи яйш нш ршиа чшу цйи лшйиа бгйи лу!
ойифшлйш яхунйиабу ёхуиаауиалс айүншчшу

цүчшхгйи эшйиагүяхшцйиа бйиыхш яуиту нүиаыхйаях ургхгй
яхуршйиаыхш ягшхү гншргхгй цүчшцйиаэйхуи ишгмш
яху ыхүгыхшойи фшлйшхйү чшйиа агйинг йшн гы шцйиа
цү ршучшй лйшчг нйү яйшчшу рш рг хгй?

ыхйиа ёш цү нүиа ншиацуи
ыхш рг гу мшйи бу ауиа нүг нш ыш лу
хйш нүг ягшхүг ншбгйи нйүчшу яхуи ыхшмгжүиа нш
яхуёш ыхшяхуияхуиабу ягшхүг ншргхгй лу

цушбуыхш жйиа яхуыхүгыхш ауиарш ыхгиёхйиа
цүнйү ёхуиачшичшу яхургхгйь чшцйиа мгёгп
цү чшхгйи яхуту чшуыхшь яхуи бу
жйихүгмй ыхшрг ёх үиач ши зйшлшу ыхгичг

冬天的匆忙
几乎无法预测:
她是一个利维亚人!
欢迎来到爱的世界

不可预知的预言
顽固的不朽之隙
天国之王
你不觉得自己是统治者吗?

你是诅咒你的人
你可以隐藏罪恶
死亡之罪是真理
你不能只是隐藏它

不管你的生活是什么
你不想打破你的怀抱
为什么不呢?
你知道怎样毁了你的生活